UNBURY OUR DEAD WITH SONG

UNBURY OUR DEAD WITH SONG

Mũkoma Wa Ngũgĩ

Abuja – London

First published in 2021 by Cassava Republic Press

Abuja – London

Copyright: 2021© Mūkoma Wa Ngũgĩ

A CIP catalogue record for this book is available from the British Library.

ISBN: 978-1-911115-98-4

eISBN: 978-1-911115-99-1

Printed and bound in Great Britain by Bell & Bain Ltd., Glasgow

Distributed in Nigeria by Yellow Danfo

Worldwide distribution by Ingram Publisher Services International

UNBURY OUR DEAD
WITH SONG

Mũkoma Wa Ngũgĩ

Abuja – London

First published in 2021 by Cassava Republic Press

Abuja – London

A CIP catalogue record for this book is available from the British Library.

ISBN: 978-1-911115-98-4

eISBN: 978-1-911115-99-1

Printed and bound in Great Britain by Bell & Bain Ltd., Glasgow

Distributed in Nigeria by Yellow Danfo

Worldwide distribution by Ingram Publisher Services International

Dedicated to Bezawork Asfaw, Mahmoud Ahmed, Aster Aweke and other singers of the Tizita.

When Tizita comes down on me,
I become a stranger to my life
And I become a vagabond and a wanderer.
—Mahmoud Ahmed

One day, I will be dead and gone
my grave untended
date of birth and death
on my gravestone from centuries past
and only my Tizita will remain.
—John Thandi Manfredi

1

'To be crowned the winner was like being named the singer of Ethiopia's soul.'

At the Ali Boxing Club (or the ABC, as we regulars called it), a metallic steel guitar, a *kora*, a *nyatiti*, a *krar*, an accordion, a regally carved antic *begena* and a *masenko* were laid out, like weapons on display, on polished three-legged ivory stools in the boxing ring-cum-music stage. There was even a dignified piano, with its black hind legs peering through an expensive-looking gold cloth, at the far-left corner of the ring. In the middle of the ring there were two 1950s silver announcer microphones, lowered from the ceiling to a chair lit by dancing, coloured stage lights. The instruments on stage formed an island, standing tall against the pandemonium of gamblers and bookies in various stages of excited drunkenness, an ocean-crowd of happiness seekers that every now and then ebbed and crashed against its shores.

Located in the middle of a nowhere that was only five or so kilometres from the city centre, the ABC was a black hole that swallowed us up, destroying our insides with expensive but cheaply priced beer and whisky, only to spit us out in the early hours of the morning. The money to be made was in the gambling, the cheap booze a lubricant between us and our money. It attracted a mixture of been-tos and those for whom Kenya was the land of their exile; *sheng*-speaking Kenyan bohemian types in permanent transition to adulthood; those from the middle class trying to climb their way up; the affluent and their expatriate friends who came down to slum and burn through money.

Something 'serious,' as we Kenyans like to say, was about to unfold. Tonight, for the first time, Ethiopian musicians were here — they were going to compete, singing the *Tizita*. The Tizita was not just a popular traditional Ethiopian song; it was a song that was life itself. It had been sung for generations, through wars, marriages, deaths, divorces and childbirths. For musicians and listeners exiled in Kenya, the US and Europe, or trying to claim a home in Israel as Ethiopian Jews, the Tizita was like a national anthem to the soul, for better and worse. As I got to learn more about the Tizita, I would understand why this competition mattered to the musicians — to be crowned the winner was like being named the singer of Ethiopia's soul.

Every musician, no matter how talented or popular, had to sing the song at least once in their career in order to be respected. It marked the difference between, say, a Madonna and a Billie Holiday. Or, even more contentiously, the difference between a Michael Jackson and a Sam Cooke. Yes, Michael was the best entertainer to ever live, but put next to Sam Cooke, something was wanting, that extra.

There was a caveat though; a badly done Tizita could destroy a career. Indeed, many flourishing careers in Ethiopian pop music had withered away after an ill-fated attempt at singing the Tizita. A musician comes along and releases a pop song that does well. He or she feels they have now graduated to singing the Tizita. But not quite. Managers and producers issue warnings, but the pop musician, adored by millions of fans, disregards their advice.... There is no coming back from a bad Tizita.

The ABC was my favourite spot — you could say I was slumming the slummers — as it was from that perverse energy that I created stories for *The National Inquisitor*, a Nairobi-based tabloid owned by a major British corporation. At the *Inquisitor*, we did not run stories about celebs living in sterilised bubbles or politicians taken over by aliens; we were not your typical Western tabloid. At the very core of a story, we worked with the truth — scandalous and salacious, but the truth, nevertheless.

Say you are the politician who uses public funds to buy diamond-studded sex toys. In real life, I probably saw one dildo and perhaps gold-plated handcuffs, but in print this becomes ten diamond-studded dildos kept in a sex dungeon. We had never been sued — in a court of law and in the court of public opinion. Would it matter just how many sex toys you bought with public funds? And if you are a Catholic priest using church money to build mansions and I tabloid your story, what little boys, now grown men, will crawl out of your cloak as the court case drags on? That grain of truth inside our stories was enough to keep the politicians, the celebs and the priests out of our way.

But really, if my friends at the ABC were to tell you my story, they would say I am the guy who accompanies the guy with the money and the beautiful woman. The foil guy, the guy in the middle of the crowd telling jokes, beers thrust into his hands; the guy who gets wet kisses from women who go home with other men. The best man at weddings and eulogiser at funerals. That my world was an open universe where people could saunter in and out as they pleased — and I welcomed them as a surrogate, temporary family. I did not mind; that is how I got my stories, being close to the action without being at the centre. So *The National Inquisitor* kept me close to the beautiful, wounded and violent heart of the ABC, and of Nairobi.

If you must think of me as I bring you this story about a Tizita competition in an illegal boxing club in Nairobi, picture me with a near-empty beer bottle in hand going up to the bar where I will find Miriam the bartender, and Miriam, without asking, will place two Tuskers in front of me. Picture me, a nondescript guy, two pens comically sticking out of my short but carefully combed afro, following old, dried and fresh blood spots to the front row seats to listen to some Tizita.

See me sipping my Tusker beer, waiting for some story or, on this night, for the story of the Tizita to unfold. Imagine a familiar feeling of suddenly being unbalanced coming back to me and my wanting to go on until I tipped on one side or the other — of something I do not know yet.

And then, much later, see me leave. I am going over to my apartment where I might or might not find Alison, my British editor at the *Inquisitor*, in bed.

2

*'It is like asking who has a better heart,
a better soul — how do you measure that?'*

Miriam liked to claim she was 90 years old, but I suspected 70 or thereabouts — when you age too fast, there is some residue of lost youth that remains underneath each wrinkle. I had done a generous story about her called "The Oldest Bartender in Kenya," and for that she always gave me a few drinks for free. First she had lost her mother to the politically-induced famine — the dictator, Haile Mengistu, had used starvation as a weapon against civilians to punish the rebels. Then, before they could have children, she had lost her husband to the armed struggle to oust Mengistu. That was when Ethiopian anti-Mengistu and Eritrean nationalists wanting to liberate Eritrea from Ethiopia fought their common enemy together, an enemy whose allegiances to the West and the Russians shifted with his fortunes. Then she lost her sister to the fratricidal war that ensued between the Ethiopians and Eritreans after they ousted Mengistu. Eventually, she was left standing alone. So she made her way to Kenya, in 'the worst kind of loneliness, of being lonely and the last one standing,' as she had described it. She had run into Mr. Selassie, and from their mutual despair, the ABC was born.

'Hey, babe, how did they decide on the musicians?' I asked her as she brought me my two pilsners.

'Nobody tells this old fool anything — it's serve beer and shut up over here,' she answered, opening one.

I laughed and made as if to walk away.

'That doesn't mean I haven't heard things though — no wonder you are such a poor reporter,' she said, shaking her head side to side. 'You know the Tizita?'

'A little bit — it's a long story, but I know the Tizita from Boston; there's a large Ethiopian community there, pan-Africanism, partying....' I answered.

'The musicians tonight, they are the best of the best,' she said, pointing at Mr. Selassie. 'He selected them.'

I started to laugh.

It was difficult to reconcile the ABC, and even more so Mr. Selassie, with what amounted to a sad, bluesy Ethiopian song. Never before had I met a man who so perfectly fit a stereotype of who he was — so much so that he begged the chicken and egg question of who or what came first. He was a short, balding man with what remained of his silky, dyed-black hair smoothed over. There was nothing as uncomfortable as seeing those stunted fat fingers jutting out of a short arm in greeting — palms permanently wet from sweat and grease, just like his real self. He was loud-mouthed, vulgar and ate and drank noisily. He wore expensive suits, and so he liked to eat wearing an apron that worked like a child's bib. It was hard to believe that he once was a promising boxer whose dreams were destroyed by the multiple Ethiopian wars.

Can Themba — the South African journalist who died by the bottle in apartheid South Africa — famously said that there are some people whose names just do not go with 'Mister', like Mr. Jesus. And there are people who go by both their names, like Muhammad Ali. With Mr. Selassie, no one knew his first name, and it just did not feel right to call him Selassie. I guess it was the respect due a man who, even in the quietest or happiest of times, was a bit scary — like the formality would someday pay off, and he would break one of your arms instead of both.

'As my people say, "Just because a man's fingers are too short to play a guitar does not mean he does not know good music,"' Miriam said, to my laughter, then moved on to another customer. That was another thing about Miriam: she had a talent for making up proverbs on the spot.

'What is Tizita to you?' I asked her after she came back to me.

'You are asking the wrong question,' she said, and waited for me to ask the inevitably right question.

'What is the right question?'

She high-fived me, laughing as her wet hands sprayed some of the soapy water around us.

'With the Tizita, there has never been a competition; it is degrading to the musicians. It is like asking who has a better heart, a better soul — how do you measure that? That is the question,' she answered.

'It is human nature — you want to know who the best is. Don't you agree?' I asked.

'We shall find out soon,' she replied. With a wink, she asked, 'You know the most important invention in music?'

'The electric guitar,' I answered immediately. Bob Dylan, moving from acoustic guitar to electric — I could not sing or play a whole Dylan song, but even I knew the story.

'No,' Miriam said. 'You are wrong — like you are always. Let me whisper it in your ear.'

I leaned in and she pulled my ear so hard that I jumped.

'What the fuck? Just tell me!' I cried.

'I just did — your ear. Without the ear, there is no music, no?' she said, laughing hard enough to need to lean onto the water-filled trough where she rinsed our glasses.

'Well, Miriam, 100 years of wisdom and you give me the chicken or the egg question?' I rubbed my ear.

'But is that really what you wanted to ask?' With that, Miriam sashayed to another customer who looked like he could use a beer.

'Why don't you just tell me?' I pleaded.

'You know those stories about soldiers stopping a war to carry their dead and wounded on Christmas or something?' she asked me as she triaged who amongst her customers was thirstiest.

'Yes, I have heard the story of how a Tizita musician stopped the Ethiopian-Eritrean war — many times in fact. But it's a myth; every major war has such a myth. A beautiful woman walking by, football on Christmas, a white dove — it's just soldiers getting tired of war.'

She reached out for my hand.

'That musician, he is here tonight — you can ask him. But my answer, you big, spoilt child, is to listen to everyone, and everything.'

She jutted her chin towards the dressing rooms.

Her smile followed my kiss on her cheek as she slipped a fifth of Vodka into my hand.

'That's on me — you're going to need it by the time the Tizita is done with you tonight,' she said, and playfully cupped a warm, wet hand on my face.

I slipped the fifth into my pocket and took a liberal, or more like a radical, swig from my beer. I did not have time to argue with her about the etiquette of pulling a customer's ears for a cliché about chickens and eggs — Mr. Selassie was walking into the ring wearing bright red boxing trunks, shoes and a robe with Ali Boxing Club emblazoned on the back.

3

'Life's a bitch and then you die.'

'Welcome to the first ever international Tizita competition!' Mr. Selassie's booming, slow-motion voice called the crowd to attention as he began explaining the rules. They were simple enough for the musicians and gamblers — winners would take it all. The winner of the Tizita would be whoever received the loudest applause. The purse was 1 million Kenya shillings, and that 'invaluable street cred,' as he put it. Finally, there was absolutely no recording of any kind allowed — and with that, disappointed faces put their mobile phones back into their pockets and purses.

Yes, a million shillings was a good amount of change, but still, why would a successful musician, one considered to be one of the best, come to a place like the ABC? I had heard of successful musicians and bands like Bruce Springsteen and The Rolling Stones occasionally giving up the stadiums and concert halls to play in small neighbourhood bars. A return to the basics, to intimate spaces where they could actually interact with and react to their audience. But that street cred, the million Kenya shillings and playing against the best — was that enough to bring an artist worth their name to a place like the ABC? Or were the musicians slumming the slummers, a two-way spectacle?

'The Corporal!' Mr. Selassie announced.

The Corporal, somewhere in his fifties, was tall and thin, with the greying but good hair that we Kenyans envied so much, smoothed back. He was dressed efficiently in jeans, a green shirt with rolled-up sleeves and sandals. His face was confident — gaunt and wrinkling, but still pulled tight by high cheekbones; he could have been an ageing runner or football player. He walked briskly and, using the ropes, he hurled himself onto the stage, picked up a guitar, and finger-picked in a way I had never heard done before — a thudded, muted yet vocal sequence of sounds that felt like heavy raindrops rapidly tapping on a corrugated iron sheet roof. A few seconds of guitar, and he picked up a masenko.

The Kikuyu people sent smoke from a sacrificial lamb high into the sky; if God was listening, it went up straight as an arrow. The masenko is an instrument of prayer that I imagine sent prayer straight up to God, but in the hands of The Corporal, the low bass buzzing notes as he bowed the one-stringed instrument were the devil announcing his presence, the sweetest, most terrifying sound.

'I have a lot to miss — but when I die, what I will miss the most is music, because music is life. When I die, I hope to ascend to the Tizita, my final resting place,' he said and then started to sing his Tizita.

He sounded like there was sawdust in his vocal cords. His

voice, trembling threateningly over the masenko, started to give way to a fear, an almost defiant fear, and several images flashed through my mind — a man at Tiananmen Square standing in front of an armoured tank; Rachel Corrie in Palestine standing in front of an Israeli bulldozer moments before the driver crushes her; Muhammad Ali, with broken jaw against Ken Norton; and, oddly, an old eagle with a stiff wing flying along a swollen and raging river before expertly diving and emerging with a fish caught in its talons.

He let out a low, long growl that went underneath the masenko, a sound I had never heard before, a voice trying to find footing from a place that was an early memory — the first sound ever made, it felt like — and then he quickly rose above, joined his masenko and closed his Tizita in his soothing falsetto.

Have you ever suddenly found yourself in the dark of the night? I mean, rural absolute darkness? I once listened to a podcast — some astronaut in space out to repair something described the darkness of space as a complete absence of light, so thick he thought he could dip his hand into it like it was oil. That was the masenko, only it was with sound.

But The Corporal was not trying to send us into space, to heaven or hell. He kept us here on our terrifying earth. We wanted to break into tears and jump into the abyss — a catharsis, of course, that would allow us to go back to the morning with all the pain and reminder it brought — but the masenko was not an instrument of flight. It was the instrument of reckoning. If you could hear your voice through the judging ears of a stranger — what kind of judgement would you give? No, we had not come to ABC to hold up mirrors. We were there to escape, and he was not letting us.

The crowd of drunks, gamblers, slummers and swingers — we his degenerate audience — we punished him with tepid applause for denying us escape. He knew what he had done to us, because he shook his head and laughed as if to say, *That was only the first round.*

It was only when he stood up and started walking to his seat by the ring that I noticed he had a limp.

* * *

'And now, ladies and gentlemen...The Diva!' Mr. Selassie screamed into the microphone.

The Diva walked in, the glow of sparkling whiteness from her diamond studded dress almost blinding, high heels tapping a confident, unhurried rhythm on the concrete floor. And all that to set the stage, it seemed, for her beauty, exaggerated by her being tall, a beauty amplified by her bright-coloured doll-like makeup. She was somewhere between caricature and performer. She climbed onto the stage and slowly wrapped long, silver metallic nails around the microphone next to the piano and adjusted it. She pulled the gold sheet off the piano, sat down and smiled as she looked at the keys. And we waited and waited, waited for a voice, for sound, that first sound, but she kept looking and shaking her head from side to side, as if the thought of playing was dragging her along against her will. She kept leaning into the microphone as if about to start singing before being pulled away by the piano.

In the audience, we started sending each other glances that betrayed our growing doubt and desperation to hear her voice, at least once — to know what she sounded like. But I was tipsy enough to let myself take in what she was offering instead of longing for what I wanted to hear. And then she fell on the piano keys, light as feathers, so that every time she hit a key my body fluttered with her every exertion. Her breath escaping her mouth in small bursts hit the microphone.

I followed The Corporal's old eagle along the tumultuous swollen river, dipping in and out of the water with her slow trance-inducing touch of the piano keys. But it felt like there was something wrong — her or me, her or the audience, one or the other was in the wrong place — and I pulled out of her world, which was really The Corporal's, and back into the ABC. I suspected this was The Corporal's doing; he had set the stage with his Tizita in a way that spoke to the musicians in a language that had gone over our heads.

She seemed to think for a minute.

'Did you know that there is no sound in heaven and space? Or words? What would music sound like without sound?' she whispered into the mic, a bit drugged, it seemed. 'And how would you really sing your Tizita? Or listen to it?'

It felt like the stage could barely contain her, and the pain or anguish of being confined seemed to rise out of her in the low cry she let out to finally start her Tizita. Yes, reading this now, you will think I am being melodramatic, but hearing that cry that started at a high note, then made lightning zigzags, tapping something here and there until she hit the earth with a bass lower than a man's — to hear that, to feel its vibrations, was to realise what not a just-failed song sounded like. It was to realise there was a lot more to her than what this stage, this night and this competition were allowing, what we were allowing. It was beautiful, this protest that hurt.

She stopped playing the piano altogether and started to sing, and even though she had stopped playing it, I could still hear it. She had suggested the piano and then let us do the rest of the work while she took us through the Tizita, filling in piano keys running fast downhill when her voice soared and letting the keys climb up a steep hill while her voice dug deep into an abyss and dragged us along and beat our bodies against its jagged edges — her glamorous look and her mournful Tizita at odds. And there I felt the tremors of extreme happiness. Then a singular force of all my tragedies — the night when my grandmother died in her sleep after a simple goodnight, my two grandfathers who died before I was born — hit me. My own weight collapsing in on me with the force of a black hole was unbearable. And then she was done.

And whatever that was, it was gone, and bewildered relief set in for all of us.

* * *

'The Taliban Man!' Mr. Selassie announced, even before The Diva left the stage. We went wild. We wanted something to wash our blood off the ring. We were not ready to go where The Diva was taking us. We yelled, clapped and patted each other, bought each other beer, lit cigarettes and nodded at each other vigorously.

The Taliban Man — I was going to ask him what his name meant to him and his fans. A name of defiance, I guessed — for an artist, it made sense — to take on that name meant to subvert its uses, whether it was the actual Taliban or the United States and its war that had now found itself in Somalia and, by extension, Ethiopia. It was the kind of name that, once you heard it, remained seared in your brain and, in time, in the recesses of your subconscious. There were the Taliban in Afghanistan and Pakistan shooting school kids in the head; there were the Americans dropping drone bombs on school kids and weddings in Pakistan and Afghanistan, and then there was The Taliban Man, the rapper musician from Ethiopia. In the ABC, it made its own peculiar sense.

Mr. Selassie laughed into the mic. 'The Taliban Man!' he yelled again.

The Taliban Man ran into the ring dressed in a black suit, a black bow tie and military boots into which his black dress pants were tucked. He did a somersault, his tall frame making it look like it was in slow motion. He walked to the piano. He hammered a few keys with youthful energy, and from the chaos, order started to emerge. Ragtime. The little I knew told me that ragtime is classical music played over itself many times at the same time — where each fucking voice has something to sing along to or eventually say. Schizophrenic classical music, but the musician has to give it form, madness contained. The Taliban Man was all of them, and I was sure he would take the cup home. He was asking us, *If you were many people with different rhythms, voices, how would you hear yourself? As one? As many?* He was playing that many songs at the same time. He hit a few more bars, leaned back and laughed into the microphone as if to say, *Just joking.*

He left the piano and picked up a guitar — he played an instrumental Tizita, the guitar clean and efficient, walking steadily underneath his voice. Then he broke into it and ran the Tizita faster and slower until he fell onto a lean, steel guitar jazz tune. It was not quite working — it was like the two were clashing, jazz refusing to be contained, but the Tizita beat insisting steadily on being heard. They both overwhelmed each other, and I for one was getting disjointed. He laughed again and lifted up his hands as if in defeat.

He paused and started a slow, major chord-driven Tizita that he drove with a hip-hop beat before breaking into rap. He rapped a few stanzas before asking us in English to clap along and repeat after him:

Life's a bitch and then you die,
You never know when you are going to go
That's why we get high on — he taught us how to pause here, letting it hang on before dropping — *love.*

We rapped along like that for a while, laughing childishly at being able to say the word 'bitch' to each other, inflected by our various accents — *mbitch, birrtch, biaaatch, bisch* and so on. Eventually, The Taliban Man stood up and led us through a roof-raising *'life is a bitch and then you die.'*

He thanked Nas and, buoyed by the applause, hopped off the stage.

4

'Tizita, What I fear the most is that
I will forget this pain that carries my love.'

We were still hungry. We were, in fact, getting hungrier. It was like they were feeding us appetizers and not the whole honey-roasted goat. We wanted more.

'And now, our very own Miriam,' Mr. Selassie yelled.

That was a surprise. Nobody, least of all me, knew she could sing, let alone compete with the best of Tizita singers. But it soon started making sense, without any logic behind it. It just seemed right that she too would be on that boxing ring-cum-music stage.

She started looking around, one hand over her eyes, until she spotted me. She beckoned and I walked over and helped her onto the stage — she felt light and frail. After she sat down, she blew me a kiss, looked up at the microphone hanging down and pulled it further down so that it was within her range. She took a deep breath, almost a sigh, into the silence that had followed her every move. At that point we, her crowd of loyal customers, came to life and started cheering her on. She raised her left eyebrow and put her right arm out, and we quieted, recognising her usual signal for when one was in danger of being cut off at the bar.

She started singing her Tizita acapella, like it was something she did every day — in the shower, humming it as she served drinks, singing it as she went about the business of living. For The Diva, The Corporal and The Taliban Man, their voices in their own unique way contained an explosive power that had to be held within the vulnerable Tizita — and their Tizita seemed to work to the extent they were able to contain their powerful range within the melody of the song, a melody that did not require one to hit impossibly high notes. They were working with more than they needed, the danger there being showing off. Miriam's voice was old, and when I listened more closely, for a moment I thought I had walked into my grandmother's house, which always smelt of wood burning, but underneath that, a warm, sweet, musky smell, like someone had eaten sweet plums and thrown the seeds and the skin on the floor in a room that rarely saw the sun. Her voice, old and hoarse from age, smoking, drinking and yelling at customers all night at the bar, sounded like the Tizita she was singing — vulnerable — and when it started cracking, I knew her voice would not carry her and us through the song.

The Taliban Man walked onto the stage so unobtrusively that it was only when he picked up the guitar that we noticed him. He gestured to Miriam to pick up the krar. She did not hesitate; they whispered something to each other, and he sat down on the stool as she went back to the microphone. The Taliban Man started tapping his hands on his thighs, tapping his boots on the wooden floor, and then he began to play.

Miriam looked at him, her smile now like that of a smitten lover. She leaned back and closed her eyes and started playing the krar, with its high and low muted strings sounding like light rain, increasing in tempo until she was playing somewhere inside The Taliban Man's guitar. The krar, in terms of range, could not compete with the steel guitar, but it could improvise, take some of the energy from the guitar, or give it largesse by letting it finish what it could not with its metallic trilling sound. The Taliban Man followed her lead and started bending his notes, but just to show us he knew what Miriam was doing, he would every now and then snap his strings so that they created a buzzing sound, like a razor bent back and let loose.

The Diva joined them on stage and started humming, a low, constant hum that rose and fell with Miriam's krar, so that they both were working inside The Taliban Man's guitar. The Corporal walked in with his masenko — the sound he lent them was no longer the anguished journeyman between God and the devil, but rather of an older, raspy and surefooted man.

I looked over at The Diva. I was expecting to see competition, or even the look that says 'I am better than them.' Instead, her look reminded me of being in primary school and that occasional class when my English language teacher, Mr. Mbugua, would say something so profound that we would look at each other in awe and appreciation. Like this one time, when Mr. Mbugua asked the most philosophical question: what if we are actually awake and living when we slept and dreaming when we thought we were awake? For months afterwards, that is all we spoke about. She had the look that said, *I am learning something, and I appreciate how it's being taught.*

Onstage, the musicians were enjoying themselves too much, and they left us behind. And by the time we caught up, it was to find Miriam playing the accordion, looking so slight and bent forward that I worried about her. But she was at it, pulling, ebbing and letting out a gentle, church organ-sounding song, the accordion lungs expanding and contracting gently, breathing in and out layered prayers. She was swaying side to side, dipping in and out, lifting one foot in and out, wading out of the river of this Tizita that as yet had no words.

She stomped her feet, ran her right hand against her left on the accordion to create confused, upside-down rainbows of sound, and then a caesura. The silence transfixed the drunkards, gamblers, slummers and the believers in place. The silence moved from being expectant to bordering on being painful. At the end of that silence where the pain was turning into relief, The Corporal with the masenko came in and bowed a long, devilish, trembling bass, low and threatening. But The Taliban Man was not going to have us threatened, and his guitar with its clean, thin sound, note for note, came in.

Miriam stomped her feet again, and silence reigned once again, and from that silence, she started singing, low, long moans gliding above and underneath the lazy accordion. The Taliban Man's guitar was getting more urgent while The Diva on the piano was furious and The Corporal on his devilish masenko held everything together.

Then The Corporal left his post and came in with the low

buzzing sound of the masenko, mourning that was amplified by the slow wail of the accordion as Miriam pulled it apart. Her voice, with a contained rasp, came in once again.

The Taliban Man did a violent lead solo. The Diva's piano jumped into the fray, playing peaceful but sharp short determined notes that threatened to undermine The Taliban Man's work. They both went on for a while as we clapped and cheered and clapped the beat.

They played on, helping each other up when one of them faltered with the beat and timing. A few minutes into the jam, Miriam looked at The Taliban Man, and he slowed down his syncopated guitar playing and the others followed suit — silence, save for the low hum buzz of the masenko and the sound of the accordion slowly running out of air.

She winked at me. 'This once,' she said in English. And she bent her voice low and joined the masenko:

When I dream of happy days, oh Tizita,
Wake me, so I can find you once again
I fear so much that you too will leave me
And I will forget
This pain that carries my love.
And Tizita, if I forget those I loved,
How can I remember who I am?
One day, I will be dead and gone
My grave untended
Date of birth and death
On my gravestone from centuries past

And only my Tizita will remain,
Only you will remain.
Tizita, What I fear the most
 Is that I will forget
This pain that carries my love

The musicians clapped for each other as we jostled and cheered for them. Some people were patting me on my back, thrusting beer in my hand, just for that little recognition from Miriam. But I was lost in one question — why had the musicians joined Miriam on stage? Had they decided not to compete? Recalling Miriam's question — maybe they had not been competing all along. It felt that way. But they could not have planned it. They could not possibly have.

Yes, I could rationalise that, in the same way I had helped Miriam onto the stage, the musicians were helping her along as well. That they too were holding her by her ribs, as the Kikuyu said of solidarity. But I started thinking through the adrenaline that was still running through me. The musicians — this I had seen — they listened, heard each other; when one of them was on stage, the others leaned forward from their seats unconsciously, tapped their fingers or moved their heads to the beat before clapping politely.

Maybe it was the nature of the Tizita: how do you compete over who is the most honest? Over who conveys the very fragility of life? Was she also right about the ear being the most important musical instrument? For now, I resolved to leave everything at call and response, the most expedient answer for

African art whenever it threw a curve ball at us.

Fuck! How do boxing-addicted, hardened gamblers listen to the Tizita without tearing into each other? No need to worry, for when Mr. Selassie said it was time to vote for a winner, we shifted listlessly, tepid applause, followed by eyes cast downwards, or lifting of bottles to lips, or people talking to each other in hushed groups, or others pretending they had just got to the ABC a few minutes ago and had no idea what had been happening. I started to feel like there were people around me, all digging and singing and dancing in quicksand, sliding into a black hole. I had overestimated our hardness.

This is what it boiled down to — there was no clear winner. It had to do with the nature of gambling; in a winner takes all, you bet on your musician and against all the others. And so you cheered your bet but otherwise remained silent. The musicians had effectively sabotaged the competition by not competing and joining Miriam for her number. And so, bets notwithstanding, to have seen what we had seen and then cast a vote — it just did not feel right. It felt downright shameful, a 'damn disgrace,' as one blues singer in Boston used to say about her cheating lover. So the purse money was going to be divided amongst them; they had created the spirit that made it possible for rules, which at the ABC were never held onto steadfastly, to be broken.

We called out for an encore, one more chance to get it right, we said, without believing that is what we wanted. But the house, which is to say, Mr. Selassie, had other plans — let the musicians go home, let them go home and work on the Tizita; in a month, there would be another round. The gamblers groaned and cursed. But the truth was that no one wanted a winner — not the musicians, not us and not the house. We wanted more of everything, and that extra that we would recognise only when we finally came across it.

I rubbed the ear Miriam had pulled — there was still a dull pain. She was onto something.

5

'A good story, like a good song, is always true.'

I knew enough about the Tizita to believe it — that the first time you heard a Tizita that was yours, you fell in love with it. You never forget your first love; you never forget your first Tizita. Where were you when J. M. Kariuki was killed? Or Ruth First, Lumumba, Kennedy or Malcolm X? Where were you when you first heard it?

For me, it was in Boston, May 5, 2001. I was at the Charles River Pub — a bar that my friend G., a fellow Kenyan and then a professor of African literature at Boston University, had introduced me to for its cheap drinks. G. was a chain smoker and, when with a drink in hand, was a master of finding deals — it was he who introduced me to Chinese wonton soup and rice all for three dollars and 'cheaper and healthier than your Big Mac meal,' as he liked to point out.

The Charles River Pub — the CRP to us because it recalled CPR — was really a depressing joint. It was largely a hangout for Eritrean and Ethiopian expatriates: teachers, students, engineers and doctors, some old enough to be in nursing homes, gambling on slot and Keno machines. The counter was like a long trough, with the beer taps shaped like bowling pins in the middle, which the thirsty lined along.

True to G.'s ability to find deals, the price of the tap Budweiser or the occasional shot of Jameson whisky were way below the regular Boston prices. But it was also the jukebox that brought us to the bar. A dollar bought you five songs, and five dollars gifted you a lifetime of revisited memories: vintage Jackson Five, Michael Jackson, Whitney Houston, Millie Jackson, Miriam Makeba, good old Hugh Masekela, Franco's ten-minute Mario, African golden oldies, and a healthy number of Eritrean and Ethiopian songs in Amharic, Tigrinya and other languages that G. and I did not speak. We would pregame at the CRP, play the jukebox, catch a good buzz and then go on to the non-minimalist but more expensive bars.

At the CRP, those mourning their bets liked to play a sorrowful, bluesy version of the Tizita that they sang along to until laughter once again filled the club. I could not understand what the lyrics meant — all I knew was the Tizita would take the people of the Horn to a place that was much more hellish than their lives, and when they returned, they seemed better. In the same way there were Lingala songs and Malian blues that I liked, danced and romanced to, but never wanted to know the lyrics — there was a risk of disappointment that I never wanted to take. This I had learned the hard way when one of my favourite Habib Koité songs turned out to be about the hazards of smoking cigarettes, a song most probably commissioned by the Malian health ministry, or worse, a Western NGO.

The patrons, noting my disinterested enjoyment, would say, 'My friend, finding your Tizita is like finding love; there is a Tizita out there for each one of us, and as in finding love, you also have to be ready to receive it,' or variations of this. And I would laugh and threaten to get my guitar and play the plaintive yet celebratory "Malaika," composed and sung by Fadhili William, who was to die penniless in a tenement slum in New Jersey while others made millions off the song — a story made for *The National Inquisitor*. As a child, I must have fantasised about being the next Michael Jackson or Fadhili William. To the failure of that end, I had over the years learned to play only one song, "Malaika." In parties, I would pick up a guitar and try to worm my way into a woman's bed by playing the song. It never worked.

It was at the CRP that I heard a Tizita that I was to fall in love with — and it was a love strong enough to mark my life with a before and after. On May 5, 2001, the owner announced that he had a new Tizita and the CRP buzzed with excitement, patrons asking who the singer was, and he telling them it was a surprise. It was a hot, muggy afternoon, but he closed the door and the windows to silence the fast-moving life outside. He turned off the TVs and keno machines. The bar went quiet when he ceremoniously opened his cash register, took a dollar and walked to the jukebox.

A murmur grew as the jukebox refused to take the crumpled dollar bill. He straightened it out by running it against the side of the jukebox, tried three times as some patrons walked over to him, waving dollar bills in different stages of crispness. He got it to work.

'My brothers and sisters, I present to you, a new Tizita by the great Aster Aweke,' he announced solemnly. There was a silence so deep that we could hear the low mechanical whine as the machine searched for the song. I had never seen something like this before. In my hometown back in Nakuru, we loved music and, in the bars, sometimes we sang along to a favourite Kikuyu pop tune, sometimes to a country song, so I was bemused by the solemn fanfare. *It is just a song.*

And then my world shifted, just like that.

On first hearing her voice rising somewhere from the clouds of a choir symphony, I felt something in me unwind. Like the sharp painful release of a knotted muscle, it kept unwinding and unwinding, until the relief turned into anguish, then as the song ended, I was left with nothing but relief, happiness even. Whatever it was, that thing that had been in me for what felt like all my life was gone.

I looked around and it was as if I was seeing the world in colour for the first time. I noticed that my friend G. had brown pockmarks on his face. On the regulars, I saw grey hairs, gnarled hands, slight flaring of nostrils; heard coughs hacking in my ears, the low buzz of activity from the streets punctuated by the roar of a motorcycle; I could smell different colognes, knockoffs of designer ones, wafting above the smell of stale urine coming from the bathroom — something in me had snapped and left me, and the same world I had been inhabiting for years became sharper and came into focus.

I pushed back my tears and went to the bathroom to compose myself. When I walked back into the bar, something strange had happened — no one was talking to each other. No one looked the other in the eye. I guess, in a way, as men and women hardened by one thing or another, we had shared too much. The owner declared one round for everyone at the bar, the spell broke, beers and whiskies were ordered, and it was like nothing had happened.

Later, when I read that when we are near death our senses sharpen, the journalist in me thought I might have been having a heart attack or a panic attack or simply a knotted muscle on my chest, something physical enough to induce or simulate a near death experience, and the Tizita just happened to have been playing. But I also knew that was the story I was telling myself.

I became obsessed. I begged for someone to translate the song for me. I bought beer and scratch-offs as bribes. And, usually, I would get someone interested; I would play the song, but somehow, the song just took over, and my would-be translator would lean back into the chair, or lean onto the bar counter and, with a slight smile of elated sadness, fold back into themselves.

'My friend, this song has no translation — you know? You must have songs like that in your language? No?' would be the inevitable response.

What does it mean? Even generally?

My friend, what can I tell you — there are no English words. The Tizita is the Tizita.

Are you telling me we feel and know differently in different languages? There has to be a way....

Well, my friend, find someone else. I have no desire to mutilate that beautiful Tizita.

And so it went on until one evening the owner beckoned me to an empty table and put a bottle of cheap whisky between us.

'I will try and help you — what do you want to know?' he asked.

'Where does the Tizita come from?' I asked him.

'No one knows, my friend — you know...maybe from our poets...in Ethiopia we are full of surprises. When Africa was being enslaved and Christianity brought to you through the barrel of a gun, we had received the word straight from God. Our Orthodox Church — straight from Christ himself! Our Tizita, who knows? It might have been around since then, before American blues, maybe from the beginning of time,' he answered as he reached into his wallet and slid a dollar towards me.

'Why don't you go and play God's gift,' he advised gently.

I walked over to the jukebox and slotted in two dollars instead so we could hear the song over and over again. I sat down, and we looked at each other through the intro of ever-falling piano keys and drums dipping in and out of silence with soft brush strokes until Aster came in and sang the first verse.

'The first two lines — she is calling for her love. Not her love, but the loss of it. She misses the pain of the loss. It is like a warm blanket. In feeling that pain, she can see her lover's face. So it is not pain or loss, but rather the memory of him.

But it is not just a memory, because she experiences the pain of that loss; she is alive again in the present with him. So the Tizita brings her lost love back to life, and it makes her sad and happy at the same time. It hurts to remember, but it is worse to heal. She does not want to heal because the wound, inside of it, is the love she lost, and it is alive,' he explained.

'And that is just the two lines?' I asked him.

'Yes, the first two lines....'

'And the rest of the song? What does it say?' I asked eagerly.

'That is all I can do for you. We love you, our Kenyan brother, but some things are for us. I cannot give it to you, because I cannot do it in such a way that will respect the Tizita, so that is all I can do for you. This is out of my respect for you. There have been some complaints. I ask you now to let the matter go,' he counselled.

'Complaints?' I asked him, wanting to laugh in disbelief.

'The bottle, it's on the house,' he said, and slid it across the table towards me.

'Can you at least tell me one thing?' I asked him.

'Anything, my brother, except that which I cannot,' he answered, pity in his voice.

'Who sang the Tizita first?'

'In Ethiopia, we have Azmaris, poets who are also musicians — a little bit like the Sudanese griots — they would move from funeral to funeral, wedding to wedding, party to party — singing praise, sometimes rebuking. It is a very tough life — but they also see a lot of life. Only one who has lived the life of wandering can sing a Tizita,' he explained. He made his way back to his customers.

So I sat there and drank myself silly. Every now and then, a patron on his way to the bathroom would gently place his hand on my shoulder. I had tried everything I could think of: Yahoo and Google, nothing; back in 2001, they were too young. There was no YouTube back then, but even years later, the comments all said the same thing to the occasional request for an English translation — impossible, it's something to do with memory, nostalgia. There was an essay by a professor on the Tizita, James Baldwin and Black American blues, and I eagerly read it, but no transcribed lyrics. At Boston University, I went to the African Studies Centre in search of Ethiopian students, but even they, broke as they were, would listen to the song and talk about everything else about Ethiopia but the song.

Desperate, I found an online international translation service, but I could not bring myself to use their services — it felt too cold and inanimate. I was desperate, but I did not want my Tizita destroyed for me to understand it. I would wait. In the meantime, I listened to that song a hundred times until, like any first love that is unfulfilled, I somehow managed to carve another life. To his credit, an amused G. helped me eat and drink inexpensively through my heartbreak.

There was a story I had heard countless times at CRP: the Eritrean and Ethiopian revolutionaries on one side, and on the other, Haile Mengistu's soldiers; trench warfare that saw wave upon wave of soldiers killing each other at close range. Then one revolutionary started singing the Tizita, and one gun after the next went silent; one after the next, the sounds of gunfire kept growing more and more distant as more soldiers strained to hear the song and silenced their guns, until the battlefield was quiet except for the singing and the groans of the wounded. As soon as the Tizita was done, the fighting resumed. Mengistu's army suffered a backbreaking defeat. *Such was the power of the Tizita,* the story would end.

I knew enough about the story to know that most cultures have their version — Christmas and the First World War, truces declared for a wedding or to bury a hero who died in battle. But every time I heard it (with variations, of course), it sounded very real. And even though I did not know it then, every time I heard the story, something in me made me aware of my own life and how little I had done with it. It made me wonder whether if someone else were to narrate the story of my life, I would emerge having at least induced one truce through some great act or sacrifice.

* * *

Once, I had got drunk with some of my journalism professors. A lot happened (and then some), just by default, with being an African journalist-in-training in a primarily white American institution. On this particular evening, the question on the table was not about fair reporting or how to write about Africa, but about how we come to write a story. Is there a story for each one of us? That only you could write, so that even if someone else came across it they would walk by it, because, for some reason, it matched your DNA? That only you could unlock?

As the night wore on and the drinks took their toll, someone said, *A good story is like falling in love — in the end, you don't know why, or whether it's worth the trouble of eventual heartbreak when your lover dies first; we fall in love and then we fight to stay in love — why that woman, or man? Why that particular woman or man and not another? No one knows. You fall in love and you become fierce — you will do anything for that love — you can kill for that love. That is all there is to it, I am afraid.* And the conversation moved back to me, and we talked about covering war and genocide.

The debate had made sense without having any meaning to me back in the early 2000s. But now it did. To be at the ABC, which I only now recognise as the Kenyan CRP, listening to the best Tizita musicians, it hit me as if I had known it all along: I wanted this story as much I wanted life. It was mine! It had waited for me to grow up.

I knew it would change me for better or worse. But if I did not write it, I would never live a full life, or write a story that felt complete. I would go through life eating honey and drinking beer and fucking with a bitter aftertaste at the tail end of everything. This was my fucking story. Let me put it this way: I had no doubt — and most journalists, at their truest, know they will do the cruellest things to get that once-in-a-lifetime story that they know is theirs.

I needed to talk to everyone. This was my story.

6

'There was going to be no objectivity on my part;
I loved it too much here.'

'Doctorrr — what can I do forrr you?' Mr. Selassie asked in a deliberately enhanced Ethiopian accent to the laughter of his entourage as I placed two Red Stripes in front of him. (People sometimes called me Doctor, or Doc for short, for the stories I occasionally doctored for *The National Inquisitor*.) He was holding court. He looked at the patron seating next to him and the man scooted over.

'Mr. Selassie, I have a favour to ask. But I have something to give, so it's not a favour per se, more like an exchange where you agree first,' I said, as he motioned me to sit.

He let out an incredulous laugh while pointing at me, at my audacity, or whatever it is that makes an upstart making a demand look ridiculous.

'Doctorrr, are you the emperor now?' he asked.

'Your competition. Give me full access and I will make the contest famous,' I said to him.

'And why would I agree? What do I get in return?' He removed his wallet to reveal it was empty. This was theatre after all, and he could not dispense favours without assuring everyone within earshot that it was hard earned.

I took out my business card and gave it to him, even though he knew what I did.

'I write for *The National Inquisitor*, and everyone who reads it — well, those are the people you want knowing about the contest, knowing about the ABC. Are you thinking music CD or video? You will need recording companies, promoters and buyers. You need *The National Inquisitor*,' I said to him.

He looked over the business card and smiled when he turned it over to find advertisements for a chicken joint — *The National Inquisitor* was cheap enough to sell advertising space on business cards. He smiled again.

'Doc, I know who you are.' He looked interested; beyond the gambling and the façade of legitimacy, he had not thought of much else, and the mention of a music album and video intrigued him.

'Mr. Selassie, it is clear to me that you love the Tizita — that you and the Tizita are one. I want to write a story about these musicians,' I bargained.

'Your name — *Doc of The National Inquisitor* — your real name, tell me again, what is it?'

'John Thandi Manfredi.'

'And what kind of a name is that for a full-blooded black African male like yourself?' he asked, sounding sarcastic and amused at the same time. He sipped the Red Stripe — a bloody good sign.

'My parents, they met this Italian doctor — I would have

died, born in the breach position with the umbilical cord tied around my neck, and so my parents…,' I cued the story for him.

'…named you in his honour,' he finished.

The truth of it was I had no real explanation as to why my parents – both of them Kenyan – would name their kid Manfredi. I had asked, only to be met with vague, changing answers. When I was younger, it was because they once had a good friend called Fred, so my name was short for A Man Called Fred. At other times, a pilot named Manfredi had performed an emergency landing on a frozen lake with a Boeing jet, a feat I was later to calculate a scientific impossibility – and so it became a landing on a busy street. In addition to Doctor Manfredi, I had several other stories, and I usually chose the one that fit the occasion best.

'You are lucky you are not Ethiopian,' he said. 'We kicked their asses out of Ethiopia – there would have been no Italian doctor to save you,' he explained, to a chorus of laughter.

'Your parents should have been cheeky and named you Menelik,' an old man wearing a Liston-Ali fight T-shirt shouted, with some effort, to more laughter. They might as well have been one person or a crowd – I just wanted to know more about the Tizita.

'Our Kenyan brother, you know Menelik?' the old man followed up.

Suddenly the whole table – all men – was throwing questions, comments and quips at me.

'A great man – a great warrior,' I shouted above them, having no idea. But it worked. And everyone at the table started speaking at once, all asking Mr. Selassie to allow me to write the story.

He stood up and shook my hand, then gave me a bear hug, lifting me off my feet so that I almost lost balance. He made a call to each of the musicians — I was to meet them one by one in their dressing rooms. And if they agreed, then I could have my story.

'Anything else, Doc?' he asked as I stood up to leave.

'Of course, there is always one last question,' I said, adopting the air of a private eye. 'How did you decide these were the top four Tizita musicians?'

I will spare you the doctor-this-and-that jokes and report to you how he explained it. He had listened to the Tizita all his life. But for this competition, he had gone to his friends, relatives, former teachers, family, artist-type contacts he had made along the way. He did as much sampling as he could — he surprised me by taking out his mobile phone, opening up an app and proudly showing me and his entourage a series of graphs and Power Point-looking statistics.

'I came up with 50, then I asked five of the people I had questioned about the Tizita to cut it down to three. They had decided on the four. I wanted three, but they gave me four. They just couldn't get it down to three. It was that simple, really,' he explained.

'Miriam?' I asked him.

'You are the doctor; see her, but be careful; she is one of the best,' he answered. I knew what he meant — I was to take her as seriously as the others; I was to be serious.

'Was it democratic? Maybe some people are better suited for judging different genres, like different weights in boxing,' I went on.

'A boxing judge can judge any weight. But let me ask you, how do you pick a judge in anything?' he asked me.

'Experts, of course. You find the experts,' I answered.

'And your so-called experts, how do you pick them?' he followed up.

'People respected in the industry....' But even as I started to explain, I could see where this was going — the judges and those who pick them, they are people who, for one reason or another, know each other. His process was just more open about it, but in the end, it really was no more or less professional than the Caine Prize or the Pulitzer — it was just as rigged or not as rigged as any of them. I thanked him and pushed the second Red Stripe towards him, like it was a treat. His entourage laughed alongside him.

There was going to be no objectivity on my part; I loved it too much here.

7

'Have you ever had to kill love?'

I started with The Diva. She was sitting on a bench in the dressing room, among the leftover boxing gear. Her perfume wafting in the room felt alien layered over the enduring smell of men and sweat. She had changed into blue jeans, a white T-shirt and dirty brown sneakers. All around her were shiny plastic bags full of clothes and other things she had bought in Nakumatt and Westgate Malls to take back to Ethiopia. She looked taller than she had on stage.

'I guess this is not exactly Broadway. Have you ever been?' I asked, half apologising for the ABC and half to talk over the awkwardness I was feeling.

'Why would I have been to Broadway?'

Her voice outside the microphone and the singing was deep, with a thin rasp at its edges; not the deepness of a woman like Big Mama Thornton, but a masculine-feminine voice — like a man and woman reading a poem together. It just sounded right coming from her. Her voice was hers.

She was not being contentious; she was genuinely perplexed.

She had her own universe, after all, as I was soon to learn. So I introduced myself and explained that I wanted to do a story on her for *The National Inquisitor*.

She stood up and reached into a carefully packed travel suitcase and pulled out a bottle of red wine, Goats Di Roam. 'South African — you Kenyans and your Tuskers,' she said with a laugh.

'We do have Kenyan wine,' I said lightly.

'Yes, just like we have Ethiopian winter-ski Olympians and the Jamaicans.... Can you just get me a wineglass?'

I hesitated.

'Okay, two!' She made a peace sign. 'And a wine bottle opener,' she added.

At the bar, Miriam seemed preoccupied, like she was still lost in her music as she went about cleaning the counter.

I held her hand to get her attention.

'We really need to talk,' I said to her. 'We just need to talk.'

'But not now.... Let me guess, wine glasses?' she asked.

'Yes, two, and a corkscrew — how did you know?' I answered, puzzled.

She started laughing and gave me two beer mugs. Why would the ABC have wine glasses or corkscrews if it was a place for the slummers?

'How did I know? What do you think?' she asked.

I understood. She was the one who made the interviews possible. The why I knew or could guess; the how I would ask later.

I went back to The Diva and gave her the bad news. She

found a pen and expertly pushed the cork into the bottle. She took the two beer mugs from me and filled them to the brim.

'Music makes me very thirsty,' she said, as she carefully lifted the overflowing mug to her mouth.

She had a slight tremor from the adrenaline of performance — I had seen it with some boxers — and a little of the red wine spilled onto the wooden floor.

'And exhausted,' she explained it away when she saw me looking at her hands.

She beckoned me to my mug, but it was so full that I first had to bend down and drink from it as if it were a trough. That made her laugh.

'Why, really why, would I agree for an interview with *The National Inquisitor*? I know the tabloid,' she said.

'I have to, I simply have to — I am in love and don't know why yet.... I just feel I have to. I feel compelled,' I said, laughing self-consciously.

'The Tizita is not a woman, or man for that matter, that you can possess—'

'I don't mean love, love,' I cut in. 'In Boston, when I heard my Tizita, I mean, I fell in love, like a haunting of something — I just want to understand.... I want to feel it.'

'You speak like a hungry artist.... I like that. I agree, on one condition: you have to come to Ethiopia. You cannot know a river by drinking its water from a glass.' She pointed to our two mugs of wine.

'Is that your own proverb?' I asked her.

'What does it matter? Do you understand why?'

'Yes, I will come to Ethiopia,' I answered. 'Before Ethiopia, one question — why did you help Miriam out? It was a competition—'

'I was not helping her. I saw a beautiful Tizita — but save all that for later. You need to see more first,' she answered.

'Have you ever had to kill love?' she asked me, seemingly as an afterthought.

'What do you mean?'

'It could be any number of reasons; the person doesn't love you back, the love is impossible — distance, or abusive. For any reason.'

'No — but I have had my heart broken,' I answered.

'It's not the same. If it's broken, it's healing. I am talking trying to kill something in you that you know is good, and as you do, you realise you have to kill something in you that you want to keep so badly. People commit suicide trying to kill that love in them. The Tizita is balm; every time you excavate, try to dig out that thing, you rub it on,' she tried to explain.

'I don't quite get it....'

'Live some more first,' she said as she stood up.

I gulped down my wine. As I left, I almost ran into a man who was walking into her dressing room hurriedly. I looked back at The Diva to see if she was okay. She laughed, either at him or me, and beckoned him in.

* * *

Armed with The Diva's consent, I made my way to The Taliban Man's dressing room. It was strewn with clothes, shoes and empty beer bottles and reeked of weed. There was a softness to him in spite of his blackened teeth and his rough exterior that I could not place. Perhaps it was a look in his eyes, or his long fingers, which on the guitar's neck were more like a spider's eight legs?

'Hey man, make it quick — I got some business to take care of,' he said, nodding at a joint in hand.

'Your stage name, The Taliban Man, what about it?' I asked him. He did not answer but gestured to his joint like he was saying, *Get on with the question.* He started to say something, but I could not make out the words until I realised he was rapping, tapping the back of the guitar to keep the beat:

I am The Taliban Man,
The Rock Man, The Caliban Man against
Which all breaks like an IED against the people,
The drone missile droning on until it hits me and
Ricochets a million miles away from home

I am The Caliban Man, bullets turn into water
Once they hit me. The missile hit the ground
Trying to drill oil but the only drilling done
Be of the people's pain and more pain,
They will drone us to death these Obamas
I am The Caliban Man and my name is your
Bane!

He finished, did a solo lead that followed echoes of his guitar rhythm before turning his back on me to re-light his joint. I knew it then, even though it was just a fleeting thought — what I had was not envy; it was jealousy. I was a journalist who wanted to be his source, to have his light and heavy coolness.

'What do you think?' he asked.

'I like The Caliban Man bit, but it sounds like it needs a little more work.' I spoke bluntly, thanks no doubt to The Diva's wine.

He turned around so that he was facing me.

'Yeah, I like you — just playing around with it. Now tell The Taliban Man what you want and get the fuck out of here!' he said.

I explained; he agreed.

'Hey man, you wanna get high?' he asked as I turned to leave.

'No, man, I am okay — the wine, Tuskers and vodka.... But can I ask you a question? Why did you help Miriam?'

'That was not help. Help is when you offer someone something. You dig? You sure about getting high, though? It will be fun: me, you, music, ideas flowing like shit, a few girls... Kenyan?' He was now pouring a mountain of cocaine on the back of his guitar.

'Have to head back home,' I said, making my way out of the dressing room.

'Well, I am gonna get high then and do my thing,' he said with a laugh.

He had, or at least his façade had, an easiness that I liked. What a guy! I mean, how cool can one human being get?

* * *

The Corporal was dressed in military fatigues, as if the man on stage had been the performer and this was who he was.

Despite the small size of the room, he had a small portable charcoal stove burning some strong incense. He asked me to sit down. I gave him my business card and explained, and when I was done, he looked at me, sizing me up. He had a bottle of Jameson whisky, thanks to the house, and he poured me a glassful into a paper cup that felt flimsy in my hands.

I did my spiel, easier this time around because I had two of them in the bag.

'I have one question for you — just for you, my friend. How are you going to write about something you don't understand?' he asked in a tone that was neither aggressive nor dismissive, as though he genuinely wanted to know.

'You mean Amharic?' I asked him.

'I mean, eh....' Unable to find the words he wanted, he simply tapped his chest.

'The heart of the Tizita?' I suggested, and he nodded in agreement.

'If you fall in love, you fall in love — everything else happens later, good or bad.' I pressed on.

He thought for a minute. He picked up the masenko and handed it to me. I felt like my hands were made out of stone.

'What can you do? Can you play your lover?' he asked.

I handed it back to him. He nodded in the direction of a guitar. 'That lover — you play?'

'I cannot play. I write,' I said. 'It's what I do.' I handed him my pen and notebook — it seemed like the right thing to do.

'You, what can you do with this?' I asked him.

'Not same.' I could tell he wanted to burst out laughing, but he held it in for an amused look.

'I mean, write me a story I want to read,' I explained.

'For a rubbish paper? Anyone can do that,' he said dismissively.

'You are wrong — to tell a good, solid lie is not easy,' I said to him.

The Diva intrigued me, and I wanted to get to know her story; The Taliban Man I wanted to hang out with. With The Corporal, I wanted to listen — it was something else, like getting fucked up with my grandfather that I never knew.

'No lies for me — I want the truth,' he said.

I flopped more deeply into my stool and raised my glass.

'A good story, like a good song, is always true — your daily newspaper contains more lies than *The National Inquisitor*. My story will have your truth, that I can promise you, and that truth will be read by over a million people,' I pleaded my case.

'I am sorry if this sounds like a...job interview — but why you? I mean you....' He looked at my business card again and jabbed a finger in my direction. 'John Thandi Manfredi?'

'Well, I have an MA in journalism from Boston University....'

'Yes, but you...why?' he prodded.

This was dangerous ground. I remembered once reading how Muhammad Ali would turn the tables and the journalist would end up revealing more about themselves than Ali. I sighed, feeling very tired and drunk.

'I am looking for something. I do not know. Okay? I am looking for something — it's somewhere in the Tizita. I am looking for love lost or found, or both.... My late grandfather and grandmother — I just do not know.'

'This story about me, the others, Tizita — is you? About you, I mean?' he asked, jabbing into my chest — he might as well have gone and pulled my ear as Miriam had done.

He started laughing, a deep, uninhibited laughter, which I was sure everyone at the ABC could hear. I put my paper cup, now half full of Jameson, on the ground and stood up to leave, feeling somewhere between humiliated and lost. I got to the door and turned around to angrily, or rather, sullenly, tell him to fuck off.

'What first?' he asked.

I was confused.

'I mean, for your story, what first?'

I started laughing, feeling like I had behaved like a spoilt journalist, more like Miriam's spoilt child, really.

'We drink first,' I said, finally finding my footing.

And so he and I sat in that makeshift dressing room, talking about the best way of telling the Tizita story. Inevitably, we came to The Diva's request — I had to go to Ethiopia. The Diva and The Taliban Man could, for lack of a better word, philosophise in English, but for The Corporal, even though he laughed it off when I suggested it, to dig deep into the Tizita as he lived it, as I needed him to, I would probably need a translator.

'Tizita — even God, every god — speak Tizita,' he had said.

8

'Love and God — they are the same thing, no?'

I returned from The Corporal to find Miriam still at the bar looking like she had never been up on that stage. And so I followed her lead and ordered my two beers, not sure how I would survive them, and stood by the counter and surveyed my fellow Tizita listeners all in different stages of extreme drunkenness.

'Jesus, go ahead and ask, and I will say yes,' Miriam finally said.

'Babe, so you sing?' I asked her, feeling my question was the understatement of the year.

'Try again,' she said.

'I mean...I feel bad. I've known you for a long time, but I did not know you could move...sing...the world,' I said.

'Much better,' she said.

She looked in the direction of Mr. Selassie. He was still holding court, so she pulled a bottle of Black Label Scotch from the top shelf and poured both of us two shots.

'Fuck. I will never get out of this club alive,' I said, as I toasted to her.

'As my people used to say, no one gets out of this world alive,' she laughed.

Miriam, in some ways, always made me feel young. She somehow made me conscious of how little I knew and how little I had done with my life, like my older conscience. Like me a few or many years from now, talking to a younger me.

'I know why I am here — in this place. But you, why are you here?' Miriam my bartender liked to ask me late into a drinking night. Coming from the epicentre of Kenyan wealth and privilege, I must have appeared to her to be spoilt, a trust fund baby just whiling away time at a tabloid.

It was not just her; my family was connected enough to get me a job at one of the major newspapers owned by His Highness the Aga Khan and could never understand why I was throwing away my life working at *The National Inquisitor*. Especially my mother, a politician who, at some point in the ever-revolving doors of who was in and out with the dictatorship, had been the minister of information, then a minister of something more obscure, then less obscure. Each of her appointments found the whole family at the State House with a small sack of money (collected from the church and other functions in the spirit of harambee), which we would give over to the dictator. Without fail, he in turn would give us sweets, Big G's, Tropical and Orbit and some cookies with orange juice before the doors were closed and the adults conversed.

My father was a retired criminal lawyer whose client list grew in tandem with my mother's rise up the shaky political ladder.

When democracy came calling in the early 2000s, they were out in the cold, but they had made enough money to ensure we could live comfortably for several generations. They were not the kind to brag about their wealth by living in a mansion manned by servants dressed in colonial era outfits, as I saw time after time in rich homes. They owned a four-bedroom ranch house in Nakuru, two cars, a Datsun Pickup and a Pajero, and a farm in which they grew flowers, mostly carnations, for export. Not opulent, considering what we could easily afford.

And then there was my brother Jack, a corporate lawyer for a major firm in the United States. He was wealthy, had two homes, one a condo in New York City and the other a mansion somewhere in Mombasa. We were more strangers than brothers; we lived in different worlds. He never failed to register his disappointment with my career path and me, especially when our parents were within earshot. And my parents never failed to talk about his accomplishments whenever we were both around, like how he had played rugby in high school, or how he was mistaken for the younger brother at family gatherings, or how he learned to save money from a young age and so on.

There was something else. Rumours. I used to hear them often — whispered in bars around Nakuru — that my mother was at some point the dictator's mistress. Someone would say that my beautiful, light-skinned mother had married a dark-skinned frog that did not turn into a prince. And when someone would point out that my father was better looking than the president and relatively leaner and fitter, a corrupted proverb about how a presidential fart by presidential fiat does not stink would be unleashed. It was not true, I liked to think, but figuratively, my mother was in bed with the dictator and, by extension, so were we all. But then again, so were thousands of other families. Far more wounding than that was seeing my parents prostrate themselves, not before God or an executioner, but before the dictator, another portly human being.

'What I am doing here?' I would repeat Miriam's question.

And then I would tell her how one weekend in 1982, my brother and I wandered out of the Intercontinental Hotel where we stayed whenever we accompanied my parents to Nairobi for one of those State House visits. We did not know what was happening exactly, but there was a lot of excitement out in the streets. Someone was shooting a movie. There were green branches from fig trees laid out on the streets, soldiers and kiosk women and men moaning in pain, some even pretending to be dead. It took us a minute to snap out of our childhood innocence and realise we were not on a movie set, and we ran all the way back to the hotel. My parents' visit to the State House had just coincided with a military coup attempt, and they were hunkered in a bunker, plotting a way out for the dictator. How naïve and protected were we?

'You are just a rich spoilt boy — the world is not a movie,' she would reply, and I would wonder what it was that connected us.

If it was guilt, I had plenty of it.

And now here I was asking Miriam to be part of my story — to let me behind the counter and into her life. I explained how I would go to Ethiopia and follow The Diva, The Taliban Man and The Corporal around.

'And then I will do you last, right here in Nairobi, at the ABC,' I said to her.

She smiled and pretended to poke me in the eyes.

'Not that easy. There is one person I want you to talk to when you are over there — my cousin. She has some things of mine that I would like back. We will talk when you get back,' she said, her voice breaking with emotion.

'Can I ask you just one little question?' I asked her. 'The Tizita, where does it come from? Someone a long time ago told me the Tizita was first sung by wandering poet musicians, like griots.' I thought back to the CRP.

'Yes, there is that — but I think it comes from the Bible. When life is really hard and you sing the psalms, when you sing to God. You cannot scream at him. You kneel down and make yourself small, and then you pray your piece,' she explained.

'But I thought the Tizita is about love?' I countered.

'Love and God — they are the same thing, no?' she asked. 'Let me make it simple, okay? Do you know when God was born?'

'No.'

'Do you have a birthday for love?'

'No. I don't understand. I need to understand.' My brain was roiling.

'You don't understand the Tizita, you feel it. Go to Ethiopia, and then we shall talk,' she said firmly.

I stood up to leave.

'Oh yeah, one other thing, babe. I have been invited to an

Ethiopian-Kenyan wedding, a few weeks from now. If you want my story, you have to be my date,' she said, coming back to her usual self.

'Free food and booze and you? Sounds good to me.' I grinned. 'Why do you think the others came on stage?' I asked her, ducking as she made a go at my ear.

'Come back from Ethiopia, then we will talk,' she repeated.

I called a taxi and filed out with a small army of the slummers, gamblers and drunks, all of them singing one song or the other that had been awoken by the Tizita musicians.

9

'We like naked things...'

I had been at the ABC all night. In the morning, still drunk in some ways and intoxicated in others, I entered *The National Inquisitor* offices and made my way to Alison's office and closed the door behind me. Alison was the epitome of nondescript — one of the thousands of British women one bustles by in the streets of London, dressed in blue jeans tucked into knee-high brown leather boots, a white sweater with a neckline low enough to reveal her blue bra straps, shoulder-length blonde/brunette/red hair disciplined by a ponytail, phone in hand and so on.

Alison used to work for a major British paper covering Africa (her title was Africa correspondent) before falling from grace. She, along with others, were caught red-handed bribing war victims for their stories. It was unfair; this was not brown-envelope journalism where a journalist gets paid by a politician. These were hungry, traumatised refugees who were telling the truth for a little bit of bread. I had done it too — a bodyguard who lives in a slum but has a story about his boss, an exploited secretary and so on. Ironically, a British tabloid broke the scandal. The owner had immediately headhunted her — entrapment perhaps? Maybe, maybe not. The point of it all was that she was not averse to a good story every now and then, but it had to conform to the tabloid genre. With slowing print tabloid sales in Britain, her boss had quickly seen what others had yet to see. The internet had yet to make its way into every home in Africa, and politics and sex and gossip about politics and sex are the only truly universal things in life. So Alison was dispatched to Kenya to start the *Inquisitor*. Word quickly spread that there was a tabloid looking for journalists to cover the wealthy sewers of Nairobi.

I had just returned from Boston, written a few pieces on spec for the national papers, but that was not the reporting I wanted to do. I had access to the wealthy and powerful. I was covering their public faces, but I knew what they did behind closed doors — from being drug and weapons mules to exchanging suitcases of public money during weddings and parties. I knew about the old men with sexual fetishes involving young girls living in penthouses they rented for them, and the men who raped their maids, impregnating them and then sending them packing. With Fuck You money and Fuck You power, they did whatever they fancied. With my mother in the government, I had a dinner seat at the table of all things sordid in Nairobi. So I went, or rather ran, to Alison. All I had to do was tell her that my mother was a former chief of justice and I had a journalism degree from Boston University. She hired me on the spot.

Alison and I occasionally slept together; a late night in the office working on a story and we would need a break. She did not ask me where I had been or why I had not called. I also did not ask her. Maximum freedom was our credo. The only thing that would matter was whether I had found a good story in the night. So I explained everything to Alison in one long drunken gush.

'This all sounds good — for *New African Magazine* or *Chimurenga* or *The Atlantic*. But here we do hard, useful gossip: corruption, sex and drugs, spoilt political kids getting high on stolen cash — you know that,' she said, opening the blinds.

Like my mother and the dictator, I thought to myself and wondered when that story would come out. Or, more precisely, when she would discreetly assign it to one of the other journalists. I did not think she was mercenary; we lived in a world where the story came first.

And the Tizita was the story I had to write. There was no way I was going to convey to her here, this early in the morning, drunk and with no sleep, what the Tizita meant, but I had to try. And I had to try it in tabloid lingua franca.

'Alison, this is going to be one hell of a story. Think about it. You remember shortly before Idi Amin invaded Tanzania? Nyerere challenged him to a boxing match to settle it like men. The Tizita competition—'

'Just how fucked up are you?' she interjected with a laugh. 'Nyerere was like four feet tall, old and scrawny, and Idi Amin Dada was, well, his name tells it all. It was the other way around — Idi Amin wanted to box Nyerere.'

'It's the principle that counts, not the principals,' I said, feeling witty. 'Imagine if all the world's problems were settled through music — you want my oil, sing better than me; you want my whatever.... At least there would be no war,' I said. 'And where there is music, there is sex and drugs, and a story,' I added when she said nothing in reply.

'Go home. Sleep. Sober up. And then give me a good reason.' She helped me to my feet and pushed me to the door.

I held on to the doorknob.

'I might have something else,' I half yelled, thinking I needed something that would speak to her English sensibilities, a vague sense of colonial guilt. Well, sometimes it's just the way to get things done with her.

'You don't care because it's African music. If I was talking about British musicians duking it out, you would care,' I said.

She laughed out loud. 'Get serious or get the fuck out,' she answered.

'OK. I have heard something, something that our readers should know about — it's like I have listened to a naked heart beating — I want to share that beat. We like naked things at *The National Inquisitor*; this is as naked as it gets. Shit, if it gets me the story, I will dig up some dirt on our stars, but this story has to be told,' I said.

'Tell me more about this naked heart of yours,' she said.

'Alison, you think you know me, but you don't. There was this story I once read by Alice Walker, about Elvis singing Big Mama Thornton's songs — you know, *You ain't nothing but a groundhog—*'

'Hound dog, you mean?' she interrupted, trying not to laugh.

'The point is that the greyhound song ended up becoming very popular, selling millions of records,' I went on. 'The Big MT gets nothing for it, but eventually, Elvis is so tortured by the singing of music he does not understand that he seeks her out. Of course, she does not tell him the secrets to her music. So, a tortured Elvis gets into drugs and eventually dies on his throne. Or some variation of the story — but you get the point. I have been moved by something — I don't want to skim on its surface; I need to feel it. And why not share that story with our readers? And you will get some amazing stories, stories that would otherwise remain buried in the sweat and the blood and the money of an illegal boxing club. Shit, Alison, isn't this what *The National Inquisitor* is all about?' I said, knowing I sounded more desperate than convincing.

'Why don't we start with last night? Write that first. If it sells, you can have your story,' she said, giving me an opening.

10

'Remember the model Naomi Campbell
and Charles Taylor's diamonds?'

I got to writing when I got home — it was a war between my imagination, drunkenness and tiredness, and an intensity that wanted more than it could have. In my write-up, I lied. I had to lie in order to be able to tell the whole story:

Sex, Drugs and Rock-and-Roll Tizita

At the popular white-and-black bourgeoisie Norfolk Hotel, a secret competition was held away from the eyes of you, the common Kenyan. It started off as a simple affair, a competition to find out who amongst top Ethiopian musicians could give the best rendition of the Tizita, a popular song over there. But, according to our whistle-blower account, once soon-to-be named Kenyan tycoons got wind of it, they decided to open up the competition to all musicians, and what was supposed to be a story about trying to find the soul in music became one of corruption, sex and drugs....

And it went on. The 'secret' competition was then opened up so as to find the best singer in the world. World-famous musicians, out of boredom and love of music, decided to join the competition. And because the winner would not be announced to the world, bragging rights alone were not a believable reward, and so I threw in ten million dollars.

I added, *Remember all the Western celebrities who like to hang out with corrupt fat cats? Who perform in the palaces and homes of the powerful? Remember the model Naomi Campbell and Charles Taylor's diamonds?*

Into this mix I threw The Diva — she especially could lend herself well to the glamorous competition, and in my write-up I photoshopped her to perfection with my pen. The Taliban Man also came out well — a Tupac, the NIC of the Tizita. The Corporal had been marched into the competition by an entourage of several soldiers; while Miriam, the sleeper Tizita musician, turned out to be from a long line of Senegalese griots who found herself born in Ethiopia because her parents had dared question the wisdom of Leopold Senghor and were promptly exiled. I turned Mr. Selassie into a suave Don King of all things illicit who had finally found the love of his life in the Tizita, injecting a bit of myself in his story.

And the judges? I hinted at a sleazy Saudi Prince who could not keep his hands off Alicia Keys. My Bill Clinton was with a young, blonde woman chewing on an unlit cigar that she would later that night stick up his ass. My Mo Ibrahim, the telecommunications guru who buys and finances presidencies, had a serious gambling problem.

But the description of the Tizita was honest, same as I have already told you: the emotions welling up in the audience as Miriam took to the stage and all the other musicians coming out to support her and to be part of her magic.

AND THE WINNER IS.... I ended the story with a cliff hanger.

My story ran one week later. For the first time in its history, *The National Inquisitor*, like a sold-out bestseller, went into a second printing. By mid-afternoon, people were calling *The National Inquisitor* asking when the next competition was going to be and if we could run a profile of the musicians beforehand. Sister tabloids in Britain and the US picked up the story. The musicians from America I had named sent in their denials. Perfect. More credibility! The advertisers were tripping over themselves. By the end of the week, I had a plane ticket to Bole International Airport, Addis Ababa, and a company credit card. I was to file a profile each week and do the write-up for the next and final competition.

There was one slight problem with my plan though — my Tizita musicians would read my story. And no talk about naked hearts and translation of the spirit would matter. I was ready. I would summon my inner Achebe and say, 'There is no story that is not true.' And hadn't The Corporal said all songs are true? I believed in the story, and as long as they saw that, the lies making the story possible would not matter. We performed to tell the truth. We would carry on.

* * *

On the evening before I left for Addis, Alison invited me to an expat party at an Ethiopian restaurant called The Nile-Not. By expat, I mean that it was like an Ethiopian restaurant in Boston — watered-down food for delicate white palates made by a white chef who had been a Peace Corps volunteer in Ethiopia, and served by white waiters. I admit to exaggerating a little bit for effect — the waiters were black. More often in American-Ethiopian restaurants, the waiters were white college students, the chef Ethiopian and the owner a white businessman who was never seen. Here in Nairobi, the waiters and the chefs and the dishwashers and the greeter and watchman at the door were all black. The Nile-Not white owner announced himself by the way he greeted everyone and the way he casually got a drink from the small bar and patted the black waiters on the back and backside.

The *doro wot* was so watered down that I gladly insulted the chef by adding copious amounts of salt and black pepper. The *injera* was a cross between thinly sliced bread and a *chapati*, none of the tangy sponginess that soaked up the goodness of the sauce. Going to the bathroom, I was mistaken for a waiter... and the indignities went on. You know how in America those in the know say there is no Chinese food in China? That Chinese food in the United States is not the Chinese food in China? But I still had booze. No worries, I told myself. What more could go wrong?

A Tizita karaoke night! When I heard the sound of the krar, for a moment I thought there was a live performer, and I kissed Alison to say thank you. Then theatre lights came on, and for the first time, I saw the stage with a microphone and karaoke monitors. Young European bohemians by night and NGO workers by day, one after the other, took to the stage and sang nightmarish District 9 Tizita. Some simply mouthed the words they were reading on the monitor while others sang their own versions of the Tizita in English. Amusing, until one American dude went Janis Joplin on his English Tizita.

'What the fuck are we doing here? Why did you bring me here?' I asked Alison. She knew about the ABC and what I was trying to do — why this caricature of my work?

'What do you mean?' she asked, smiling.

I stood up to leave in meaningless protest. She was driving. I sat back down, my face saved by the arrival of my beer.

'They too have stories. I wanted you to see that — a story can be in what you do not know, right?' Alison said as she leaned in closer.

She was right, of course, but their expat stories were not for my pen.

We stayed for a while, went to my place all fucked up. She watched me pack, and then guiltily, or perhaps out of obligation, we had sex and slept.

11

The Diva

'How hungry are you?'

I was finally in Addis, standing outside the Panorama Hotel waiting for The Diva's driver. I felt a tap on my right shoulder. *Surprise!* It was The Diva, playfully peering over my left shoulder, looking almost unrecognisable, and it took a few seconds to figure out why.

In Kenya, she had been wearing the armour of a foreigner, the same armour that I would feel enveloping me whenever I returned to Boston from a visit to Kenya. Nothing distinct or pronounced enough for you to complain about, just a general awakening to the life outside of what you know — made worse by the nascent feeling you are not entirely welcome. The letting go of the armour, the relief, is not through conscious effort either and is never pronounced enough to be articulable, but I could recognise it in her.

I did not have time then to think it through, of course. Here you have to see her marching off, gesturing to me and pointing at an Oldsmobile-looking blue taxi and see me hurriedly walking towards her. By Oldsmobile-looking, I mean it had

the sharp architecture of cars made in the 1960s — the kind
you would see in a post card from Cuba. She helped me load
my bag into the boot, even though I did not need her help. She
belly-laughed till she snorted when I clutched onto my carry-on
with my laptop (a hand-me-down from my mother or father)
and recording equipment.

'That nervous twitch — it makes you a tourist,' she said,
pointing to my hands. She did not sound judgemental, more
amused.

'Relax, man, you are still in Africa,' she added.

'My point exactly,' I said, to more of her undignified laughter.

To be fair, I have known many African musicians who are
famous and have sold a million records but still take *matatus*
and eat Kenchic chicken like the rest of us — victims of bad
contracts. But The Diva — I had read and seen enough of her
to know that she was far from being broke or exploited.

Everyone called her The Diva, but our mutual friend Google
had told me that she had undergone multiple plastic surgeries,
her real name was Kidane and she owned her own recording
label, Guava Jelly Records, named after Bob Marley's poetic
love song, "Guava Jelly." Her concerts in Ethiopia routinely
sold out, and she had her own Guava clothing line and a Guava
Diva perfume. In other words, she was, in addition to being
incredibly talented, a savvy businesswoman. I could not help
but wonder where her entourage and limousine were. But here
she was, squeezing with me into the back seat of the bright
blue, unforgivingly hot taxi. The question lingered as the torn
vinyl covering the back seat bit sharply into my butt.

'How hungry are you?' she asked. I looked at the time: 9.15am. I had just had breakfast, and I was feeling hungry again. But it was the kind of hunger without an appetite — I was a bit apprehensive — so I said no.

'Coffee then? Have you ever had Ethiopian coffee before?' she asked.

'No, and I am really okay,' I said, feeling less like a journalist and more like a guest.

The roads in Addis were empty, which allowed me to look at the quiet architecture. It was like Nairobi, or London, like any other city where the language of global capitalism glitters with the same sort of opulence; billboards that, like pictures, speak a thousand words more than the Amharic I could not read — Nike, Timex, Heineken, Volvo and others. We drove by a Bob Marley statue and then the African Union headquarters, a building that is really a billboard for an Ethiopia on the march to a heaven paved with gold — only it was built by the Chinese.

Addis was much greener than many cities; it was as if it was carved out of a forest, and there were still patches left every few blocks. In Nairobi, a tree outside the designated park is as rare as a non-corrupt policeman or politician. In Nairobi, traffic lights outnumber the trees ten to one.

A few kilometres out of the city, the vegetation became a few patches of green shrubs rising out of the suffering, tall, green and brown, alive and dying grass. It was not exactly a desert, but it was close to being one.

To amplify the loud language of globalisation, we soon came across a slum: muddy with dog shit and rain; little children running around having fun with homemade toys of all kinds, from guns to footballs; women and men, presumably their parents, engaged in small businesses selling vegetables, illegal alcohol, mobile phones and glittery knock-off Citizen watches and Clive colognes. It was in sharp contrast to the quite empty and spacious Sunday Addis. I was not being judgemental — I am Kenyan after all — just pointing out our similarities. I looked over at The Diva and she shrugged. I did not ask why.

All along, The Diva had been chatting with the driver in Amharic, every now and then breaking into laughter.

'We have better food here,' the driver said in English as he twisted his neck to look at me.

'I was a refugee in Kenya when things were bad here, but the food there made me so miserable I came back — a life of boiled maize and beans and tough, very tough, goat meat. A life without doro wot, who wants that?'

'I must defend my Kenyan friend,' The Diva said. 'It's as the good Lord Jesus said, "Forgive them for they know not what they do."'

'That is not much of a defence,' I pointed out, smiling.

'For they do not know the shit they eat is more like it,' the driver said.

'Someone's doro wot is someone's....' I could not think fast enough to finish the proverb I was trying to make up, and we laughed. The Diva was surprising me in all sorts of ways.

The taxi eventually came to a stop, and she explained to me that the driver could not drive any further without ruining his car. We had to walk the rest of the way, 'a kilometre or so,' she assured me.

It was about 10am — the heat from the sun was at a perfect pitch, just hot enough for me to feel the hair on my forearms bristle and cool enough for my skin to want just a little more heat. I found myself looking forward to the mid-morning walk as we started up a hill, the thin brown grass broken into tracks probably used by a donkey cart. After thirty minutes of staring at a monotonous grass path that would not quit, of trudging up and down hills and valleys, my luggage in tow, I was labouring for breath — thanks to all that ABC living. She took my duffel bag; I protested, but not hard enough. She slung it across her shoulders, and we kept walking. About halfway over yet another hill I slowed down to catch my breath.

'Maybe the city boy would like to sit?' she asked me with a half-amused look on her face, soaking wet with sweat as I was.

'Maybe for a minute.'

I sat on the grass and she on my duffel bag, and I found myself worrying that her sweat would soak into my clothes.

I took out my small recorder and mic.

'Talk for a minute or two?' I asked.

'Anything to catch a break?' she asked in turn, but before I could respond, she was up and walking.

'I want you to write about what you see, not what I tell you. No one taught you that?'

All my energy was now going into keeping up. I could not respond.

On top of a hill, we came across an old man standing by the bend of the road, reading something and then chanting into the wind, every now and then picking at the grass and throwing it up in the air. I looked at The Diva.

'Kidane!' the old man called to her. She waved, and he continued chanting.

'By the way, out here you should call me Kidane,' she said to me as we walked on. I asked why, but she did not answer.

'The old man? Should we not have stopped?'

'You want to rest again? His son died years ago; he was a soldier. Each year he does that, so we let him,' she explained. 'But this hill, this is where they spent most of their time when he was a young boy herding cattle, so he comes to remember. Even the hills sing the Tizita.'

'Kidane, did you know him?' I asked.

'Yes, as kids we were close. Look, just keep walking, okay?'

And so I did as we fell back into silence, walking another ten minutes or so until we came to a farm.

'Home,' she announced as she opened the gate, or rather dragged a metal sheet to one side and walked in.

Two little kids, about ten, give or take — a girl with a massive afro and a boy with closely shaved hair, both with missing teeth — ran out as soon as they heard the gate.

'Mummy! Mummy!' they yelled as they hugged and dragged her along.

Staged? Definitely staged for the benefit of the journalist, I told myself as a tall, thin man with a doctor's bag walked towards us looking at his watch.

He leaned in and, with practiced efficiency, kissed her. 'I have to go see...' He gave a name that I did not catch.

'My husband, Mohamed — a doctor,' she introduced me.

'A doctor with a patient he has to go see,' he interjected.

'And this is the journalist,' The Diva continued.

'I thought we agreed!' Mohamed said to her as we shook hands.

'No, we never really agreed — it was a truce,' she answered.

'In a truce, you sneak him in?' he asked, and laughed to himself.

He looked at his watch again and said something to her in Amharic, which I guessed to mean, *We shall talk about this later.*

He kissed her on her cheek and left.

We walked into the house and she showed me around; her two kids excitedly pointed out things like windows and doors. They named the girl Selamawit to mean she is peaceful and the boy Tsage to mean happiness, she explained. They lived in a five-bedroom house — well-maintained, but over the years, the wear and tear had caught up with it. The fresh coat of beige and brown paint could not hide the rotting wood planks, and the furniture showed just how busy the two kids were. The one thing that stood out was an electric keyboard sitting in a small room with nothing else in it besides a chair and expensive-looking DJ headphones. She showed me the rest of the house, including a small guest bedroom that overlooked rows upon rows of hills. 'Some of which you met,' she pointed out with amusement.

I promised myself I would be seated by the window later, in the night, staring into the darkness, conjuring up the hills in my mind and writing.

12

*'Now, tell me, are you the spark that lights a fire,
or the spark that the fire throws out to die?'*

By mid-afternoon that first day, I could tell I was going to love being out at The Diva's, aka Kidane's, farm. Our house in Nakuru was not really a farm — it was where we that were privileged enough not to need farm animals lived. On holidays, we would do what city families do and go visit our rural relatives in Limuru. We would bring all sorts of gifts, from mirrors to clothes, and they would slaughter a goat for us. An envelope would change hands, promises would be made that they would send the kids to spend a weekend and get back to their roots, learn how to speak proper Kikuyu, and then we would retreat back to Nakuru, where my mother, feeling inspired, would start a vegetable patch that inevitably went to weed.

Being out here, with the familiar pungent smell of cow dung permeating the air, the grass still soft from evaporated morning dew, was awakening a need to reconnect with Limuru and the relatives who over the years had become just somewhat familiar faces.

'Mummy said we should not disturb you, but she always

sleeps when she comes back,' Tsage said, looking sad. The kids were now in my room as I unpacked.

'Well, sometimes grownups work too hard and they need to rest,' I said to him, but he looked at his sister.

'Singing is not hard work — do you want us to sing you a song so you can see it's not hard work at all, at all, at all?' Selamawit asked, getting ready to belt out a tune.

'No, no, I believe you. Maybe later? Later would be good,' I said to escape.

'Can we show you the farm now?' she asked. I supposed this was the real reason they had come to see me.

So we went around the farm; one moment they would be pointing out in perfect English what we were looking at — chickens, cows and goats — and the next moment they would play jumping and skipping games that I did not know. We got done with the farm and went back to the house only to find that Kidane was still sleeping. But at some point, she must have gotten up, because someone had set out some marmalade and jam sandwiches, some milk and a Fanta, and so we snacked away.

'Now is later. Can we sing now?' Tsage asked.

I pretended to think about it as I sipped my Fanta and, of course, said yes. They danced and sang to Michael Jackson's "Beat It." Did they have their mother's talent? It was too early to tell.

It was time for me to be a journalist. While The Diva slept, I would walk around with the hope of seeing something that might be useful for my story. After all, she wanted to show, not tell.

The kids wanted to come with me; I agreed, thinking that they might be useful guides and could translate for me if need be. I packed the rest of the sandwiches in a brown paper bag I found in the kitchen, filled an empty juice bottle with water, and we strode off into the hilly great unknown.

The kids skipped ahead as I took in the view and wondered who The Diva really was. So far she had introduced me to her family, her house and farm and then napped. Peace and happiness, she seemed to have it here. But how can you sing the Tizita if you have everything? If blues musicians did not have loss, would they sing? Can you sing and be spiritual about the loss of something you have never known?

There was a sound that for years had bothered me from my days in Boston watching blues musicians. The sound of their wedding ring running against the frets — did that mean they were still married even as they sang about loss? Now I was thinking that one probably sings a truer song about loss when still in love — the anguish, the imagining that you will lose the love of your life. Otherwise, after the love is gone, the bitterness, anger and pain would choke the beauty out of the song — and it becomes longing for love once again.

We went down and up a hill, and I found myself thinking about the chanting old man. And, as if I had conjured him, there he was, still chanting. We walked over and stood close to him until he acknowledged us. He stretched his hand in greeting and introduced himself.

'His name is Giriama Felleke. And you, who are you?' Selamawit happily translated.

I told him my name. He wanted to know a little bit about my background, why I had an Italian name, telling the kids to tell me that even a fruit that falls down from a tree still has roots. I had to think fast which of my myths of origin would work best, and I went with the pilot who had landed his plane on a frozen river, and my mother, pregnant with me, giving me the name of the pilot who had saved both our lives — Manfredi.

'They should have named you Tamru — it is a miracle, God's will, that you are alive,' he said with great empathy. 'And your middle name, what does it mean?'

'Thandi — it means spark.'

'Now, tell me, are you the spark that lights a fire, or the spark that the fire throws out to die?' he asked, looking pleased, like one who had been dying for a conversationalist and had now found one worth sparring with.

'Well, either is fine by me — either the piece that gives greatness or the piece that comes from the whole — either way, I am fine,' I answered, and he started laughing.

'I am a journalist; I am doing a story on Kidane. Do you mind if I ask you a few questions now that we have sparked a conversation?' I asked.

He laughed so hard I thought he would fall and roll down the hill. He whispered something to my able translators.

'He would like something to drink. He has been here too long,' Selamawit translated.

I gave him the water, but he shook his head to say no. I figured the kids would be okay. I ran all the way back to the house, thinking about my name and why it mattered that my parents had been in bed with the dictator.

This is the version I never told anyone. My name was suggested by the dictator — an inside joke. It's the name of the hotel where their affair started when he was the VP and my mother was coming up the party ranks. No, I was not the ex-dictator's son, though I always did feel he favoured me. I was a reminder of simpler and perhaps happier times. Why had my father gone along with it? For the same reason as my mother — it made him part of a club, and, in his own way, he might have felt it was something he held over their heads.

How did I find out? The dictator's sons had told my brother, who in turn had taken great delight in telling me. I had doubted it and looked up Manfredi Hotel, and there it was — a small boutique hotel in Rome. I asked my mother if she had ever stayed at a Manfredi Hotel in Rome. She said she had never been. But old passports do not lie. And neither do archived newspaper reports of official government visits to foreign countries. Everything — the lies and truth, or truths — was possible.

The Diva was still sleeping. I found a bottle of vodka that was clearly old, judging from the dust it had collected, and ran back to the old man. He motioned for us to sit down for a ceremony that only he knew. He poured libation after libation, taking a gulp of the vodka and spraying out a small fine mist. I had to get my questions in before he passed out.

'Can you ask him if his thirst has been quenched?' I asked my little translators.

'Yes, I am very fortunate. I am ready,' the answer came back.

'The chanting, who is it for?' I asked.

He hesitated. 'The problem, some stories are not for young ears,' he answered, and laughed.

I understood; my translators were too young, even if only transmitters. I took the bottle from him and had a good swig and gave it back to him.

'Tell him, I am old enough for him to tell me the story without really telling it to you,' I answered, thinking of the heavy Kenyan code that old people would use in our presence — ordinary words that, used in a certain way, had so many meanings that they must have had a code to decipher. They were the original deconstructionists and post-modernists; only, they had meaning.

'Life is long, life is short. It's longer for others and even shorter for others, and even a long life can be short. When people do not get along, we send our children to help settle the debate and some come back, and others trip, fall down and decide to stay. My boy went back to our neighbours to help settle a little disagreement. He was lucky to come back, but if you go somewhere to visit, sometimes that place makes you a different person....' He paused as my translators intervened.

'His son came back from the war with Eritrea. He was crazy — he blew his brains out right here,' the sister explained as the brother made a gesture of holding a gun to his head. I looked at the old man, thinking he might be angry, but he smiled and lifted the bottle to his lips.

'The young of today, we can't get anything past them,' he said and patted them on their heads. 'But they also don't know everything,' he added.

Now that the children had broken our code, I felt reluctant to ask him about Kidane, but I risked it anyway, hoping he could launch both of us into deeper code.

'The mysteries of the heart. To tell the truth is very difficult work; the truth is like hot lava going through the musician. Even if they try, it will still burn and leave them with scars. But it is also beautiful work,' he said.

'Sometimes my mother drinks too much and then fights with my father,' the little girl once again injected her two cents into the translation. The old man laughed again. He must have understood English.

'Perhaps we are saying too much?' he asked rhetorically, but it was too late for him to stop. 'Kidane sings for my son, to bring him back. Anytime I hear her sing, I can see my boy right in front of me, but each time, we are not the same after – and so I take a little medicine,' he carried on.

This is what he is telling me, I think – *Kidane and his son had been lovers, were probably going to get married, but he came back from the war traumatised. Her love could not save him from the ghosts of war that were calling him over.* The landscape, this place, was not so full of happiness and peace after all.

'The war between neighbours, between Eritrea and Ethiopia, what was it about?' I asked him.

'War between brothers never has a reason – the brothers of Pakistan and India, Bangladesh; the brothers of Britain and France; the brothers of Kenya and Somalia. We have been killing our brothers for too long,' he explained, suddenly looking very close to breaking down.

I thanked him. He went back to his chanting, and we started our walk back.

'You are the reporter writing about my mother, right?' Selamawit asked.

'Yes, he is. You know he is,' Tsage answered for me.

'You must be very special,' she said.

'Why?' I asked in surprise.

'We never meet any reporters,' she answered.

'It must be because your mother and father love you and want to protect you from being known to strangers. Imagine how difficult your life would be if everyone in Ethiopia and the whole world knew you...,' I awkwardly tried to explain.

'It would be very, very nice to be famous,' the boy answered eagerly.

'But how would you know if your friends loved you for who you are?' I asked both of them. God! How many times had I asked myself that same question growing up?

'I would not care at all. I would make them do what I want. Why would I care as long as they did what I wanted?' Tsage reasoned.

He had a point there, I guess — it would be nice to be able to bend the world to your will.

'OK, in that case, let me take a photo of the both of you, but I will ask your mother for permission to use it,' I said, to close the subject.

I took the photo, knowing I would not use it, and they skipped and hopped ahead of me till we got back to the farm.

13

'I have many answers, but here is one.'

Kidane was up and in the kitchen making tea. She was dressed in the kind of outfit that I have long associated with old African women — a dress decorated with flowers, and a loose waistband that made it formless. She could tell what I was thinking because she said, 'It is, as a matter of fact, very comfortable.'

The kids went outside to play. She turned off the gas stove and got out a bottle of Red Label and two glasses from a cabinet and asked me to follow her outside, where we sat on the long veranda. Looking down the hill, I felt that if I were tall enough, I could dangle my feet in the air.

It was time.

'Why don't we start with your parents and then talk about your childhood?' I asked her. She threw her hands in the air, walked back to the house and came back with a green photo album and sat next to me, so close that I could smell her worn-out perfume and bad breath fighting its way through the sharp smell of the scotch. She showed me old black-and-white photos of her parents. Her mother had been the headmistress of the school where her father taught English. We kept flipping through the photos; her parents got older as she grew from a toddler to a teenager to a young woman on her wedding day to a mother holding her first child. They aged with each flip, until they died of old age. There were no photos of a young Diva at a recital or playing the piano or pretending to sing and dance with a fake microphone, nothing to suggest an early interest in music.

'When did you know you wanted to be a musician?' I asked.

'I did not know my parents could sing, I mean, really sing, but on my first day at school, they came to my class and taught us how to sing the national anthem. They did a beautiful duet — that was the first time I knew I wanted to be a singer. The national anthem...I did not know it then, but what I was responding to was the soul, the blues in the anthem. Know what I mean? There is a deep longing in our anthem, like a Black American spiritual,' she said and started humming the anthem.

'What do you mean?' I asked above her hum.

'The anthem is about love and light, love and truth; God's children wailing from distant lands; humanity, not just Ethiopians, but all of us, pleading — that was the old anthem where we prayed to the Emperor to protect us. Fuck the politics of it all, it had soul, something about the way the words were strung together. A song, the way it sounds, can have a different meaning from the lyrics. I did not hear Emperor Haile Selassie. I did not hear politics at all — I heard a need to be with others. What I remember is my mother and father looking like young lovers. Singing made them beautiful — it was almost like they were singing a love song. It *was* a love song....'

I could see my story forming already — the first sentence in *The National Inquisitor*: *On that beautiful morning when a wide-eyed, young Kidane (she was not yet The Diva) heard her teacher-parents sing the national anthem in front of the whole school, it was as if she was hearing her calling. But not a calling to God or to country, but to connect people through music.*

'Did your parents sing at home?'

'No. Never. Not once. At home, they watched TV in the evenings, marked exams and prepared for school or worked out in the garden. I don't know what home was to them, and by the time I knew to ask that question, they had passed on.'

'Did they know you could sing?'

'They neither supported nor discouraged me. They knew what I was doing; their plan was to let me grow with gentle guidance, my father once told me — and whether I became a flower or a weed was up to me. I was complaining to him as a child that they did not care about me,' she said with a laugh.

'It must have been extremely lonely,' I said to her, trying to mask the pity in my voice with journalistic curiosity.

'To the contrary. I could do anything and go anywhere. I was my only limit. Can you imagine that? They loved me, and so they let me grow into myself. I could do wrong, but there was no one to punish me, and it became easier to do the right thing. I try to do the same thing for Selamawit and Tsage.'

I could hear the pride in her voice.

'Can you give me an example?' I asked.

'I started smoking cigarettes when I was 12. They knew but did not say anything. Instead, they started giving me more money for lunch, and so I quit smoking. Call it reverse psychology. Or sex — I started having sex when I was 14 with a 15-year-old boy. I wanted to. My own terms. No sexual hang-ups for me,' she answered.

'Did they know?' I asked her.

'I don't know if they knew about the sex, but they never stopped us from seeing each other. The old man — that was his son,' she explained, her voice dropping so low that I heard echoes of her performance at the ABC.

Yet another juicy bit that I knew would be good for my readers: The Diva, intellectually emancipated at birth, sexually liberated at 14, owned her life from the day she was born, thanks to her anarchist parents. She meets a boy. They fall in love. He goes to war, returns and shoots himself in the head.

'You know what they used to call me?' she asked, as she placed the album on her thighs and rested her hands on it.

I had no idea.

'The boys from around here — even some record execs — called me Buck Horse 'cos of my teeth — the front four,' she said, with the pride of someone who had overcome her past and triumphed over her enemies. 'The first thing I did....'

Somewhere deep down in her voice, I thought I sensed a tinge of regret.

'Surgery?' I asked her.

She shook her head to say no, her eyes falling on a photograph.

I looked at the photograph closely. I looked again and looked at her — she wanted me to see it: she had not had surgery.

'Why?' I asked.

'You mean how, you should ask, how?'

'How?'

'I did nothing, just improved...completely redid the way I looked — hair, dressing, make-up. Disguise is the simplest of all things — in my case, I became the face of the voice they wanted to hear. The first thing I did when I made some money was to buy The Diva. Money is all it took,' she explained.

'No one noticed?' I asked.

'No one looked hard enough — they see glamour, the diamonds,' she explained. Once she became The Diva, her long hair draped on her shoulders, all glitter and voice, she became what people wanted to see.

'But why didn't you get them fixed? It would have been easy enough,' I pressed.

'What if it changed the sound of my voice?' she asked in turn. 'Do you play anything?'

'A little guitar,' I answered, knowing what was coming next.

'Then you must play me something,' she said as she went in to get a guitar.

She came back with an expensive-looking acoustic electric Fender that, like the keyboard, seemed out of place out here on the farm. The kids, on seeing the guitar, joined us.

I had sung "Malaika" a countless number of times, drunk at BU student parties, in the perpetual hunt for a one-night stand that never materialised, but never for a musician I was interviewing, and in front of her two kids on a farm deep in Ethiopia. I found myself, as I explained the song to her, thinking about it in ways I had never before.

"Malaika" was, in a way, our version of the Tizita, a Kiswahili version. In the song, a man cannot marry the woman he loves — he doesn't have the money, presumably for a dowry, but also to make a home. But it's more than an absence of money; it's an absence of a fortune. *Can you have a lot of money but not a fortune?* I wondered. He blames her for turning down his proposal even as he yearns for her. The young man in the song has faced adversity in his quest for a fortune and he has lost, resulting in a double tragedy — loss of two things yet to be acquired. He loses before he knows what it is he is not getting. I asked if she thought "Malaika" was the Kenyan Tizita.

'I have many answers, but here is one,' she said as I laughed. 'Tizita is of a love lost a long time ago — before you are born. Let me put it this way, "Malaika" is the song the original Tizita singer sang when the wounds of losing love, country, parent, sibling — of losing life while still alive — were still fresh. All those losses over years become something you pass on from generation to generation — the moss of all those broken hearts and loss gathered in a song. "Malaika" is the fresh wound; the Tizita is the scar. "Malaika" has a face; the Tizita is faceless, or rather, it has so many faces that it is faceless.'

I could see that there was something very old that the Tizita invoked in me that I could not name yet. I started playing, but she declared the guitar out of tune, taking it from me to tune it herself. Kidane, of course, knew "Malaika" — the chorus at least — and so she joined me, her voice making mine sound even more out of key, but I could tell she was having fun, so I kept playing, repeating the chorus at every opportunity. She went in and came back with another guitar and started strumming along with me. She quickly mastered the three chords so that, in a little while, she was picking the strings with her fingers while I strummed.

We played for a while before I asked her to show me how to play the Tizita. A few complicated chords and I gave up, so she offered to teach me how to play a simple bass line, repetitive and soothing, like the hum of a nearby stream, while she played the rhythm. The kids went and brought small drums and the band started warming up. After trying to have me follow her, she gave up, took a hold of my fingers and guided them through the bass line as she hummed it. Finally, I got it, and we started playing and getting into it until her voice was soaring so high, or rather gliding up above her guitar, above my awkward bass line. I could almost see the sound waves separating, her voice going higher and higher while the guitars remained constant, like a beam of light coming out from where we sat going into the sky, getting wider and wider. She kept getting higher and higher until we lost the song, and we sat there laughing.

'Now you see why the Tizita is not about the voice but containment,' she said, slightly out of breath. 'The explosion is in the containment.'

The concert continued as the kids crowded around her and demanded the guitar and plucked away at various Ethiopian lullabies. It was soon time for them to go to bed, and Kidane went in to feed them and tuck them in. I was left to my own devices, consisting of a half-drunk bottle of whisky and a guitar. I sat there plucking away at bits and pieces of songs, trying to string the Tizita to "Malaika."

14

'Well, sometimes beauty is not comfortable.'

Kidane in the kitchen was pure chaos, pots and pans all over the place — and in the end, dinner was spaghetti and tomato sauce. She had a concert the following day, she said, to explain the haste. Her kids ate away, as I did — spaghetti and tomato sauce was one of my favourite dishes as a kid.

I went up to my room intending to write, but after an hour or so, I gave up — I had not seen enough. There were some nascent questions, though: what kind of an African middle class doesn't have kitchen help? Or a watchman to stand by a gate? What was it I was missing?

I undressed, hopped into bed and tried to fall asleep, but I was exhausted — the kind of exhaustion that makes sleeping impossible. I called Alison only for her to sleepily tell me to fuck off.

A stiff drink seemed like the next best thing. On my way to the kitchen, I noticed the light was on in the small room with the piano and decided to turn it off. But Kidane was in there, stark naked, headphones on, playing a song I could not hear.

'In space and heaven there is no sound,' she had said back at the ABC. This was as close as I was ever going to get to hearing, or rather witnessing, music without sound. I did not dare enter to disturb her, so I just stood there observing a naked woman, her hair down to her back, her statuesque figure shaking gently, and other times violently, as her hands moved across the keyboard, sometimes so forcefully that I could feel reverberations on the wooden floor and up my naked feet, and other times so softly that all I could hear was a light flutter. Sometimes, she would hum, but without the music, the melody sounded disjointed. It was like watching a painting come alive.

I could get why she was playing late into the night — but naked? To stand naked before the Tizita? To share vulnerabilities? To feel it on her skin in a way that she could not in front of an audience? Or was it just too hot, and she thought I would be sleeping? Or was it my dream?

I could have stood there and watched her for hours, but I heard the key turning. It was her husband returning, and, understanding there would be no easy way to explain why I was standing there watching his naked wife play soundless music, I took that as my cue to quickly but quietly go back to bed.

I soon heard his footsteps pause by the music room. They were talking, and in spite of myself, the tabloid journalist in me was curious enough to decide to eavesdrop. What kind of a conversation would I have with, say, Alison if I found her stark naked writing on her laptop? What was I thinking? Of course, they would speak in Amharic. I lost interest and went back upstairs. I heard their laughter followed by lovemaking amplified by the increasingly urgent creaking floors.

It was funny: seeing her naked had not turned me on; it hadn't even occurred to me — I would say it was sensual or, more accurately, sensuous without being sensual. But now, hearing them making love, there was nothing to do but to masturbate along, matching their intensity, so that we all came together.

What must have been an hour or so later, I heard giggles by my door. I thought the kids were up for some reason. I put on my boxers and opened my door, only to find both Mohamed and Kidane beside themselves with laughter. They were standing there doing rock, paper, scissors to see who would knock on my door. They were clearly tipsy, and I tried to show my annoyance by letting out a loud yawn, to which they laughed even more.

'Come on, you know you want to join us! Put some clothes on, we are going to start a bonfire. You can help,' Kidane said and dragged Mohamed down the stairs with her.

We piled up a mountain of wood and brush. One slight problem, it was all mostly damp. Mohamed had an idea; he had some petrol in the shed. He fetched it and liberally poured it on, struck a match and threw it onto the brush. Terrible, stupid idea! An explosion! I have never moved so fast, or seen other people move even faster. We sprinted off in different directions and congregated back when it was safe. They were drunk enough to find it funny — who ran faster, the Kenyan or the Ethiopians? Adrenalin still coursing through me, I took liberal swigs of whatever bottle they had thrust into my hands.

Luckily, the tired kids (thanks to me) were completely wiped out and did not wake up.

The fun had just started. We kept adding more wood and brush; the bonfire crackled and snapped, and we kept moving back the perimeter until it felt like we were standing a kilometre away from a small, angry, erupting volcano.

'It's a thing of beauty!' Mohamed said in admiration of our handiwork.

'But it is so damn hot!' Kidane, now more like The Diva I remembered, echoed my thoughts.

'Well, sometimes beauty is not comfortable,' he said, passing a bottle of Scotch to her.

'Getting a bit philosophical?' she asked, sounding annoyed.

On my way to sudden drunkenness, all I could think was that something had been brewing between the two of them.

'No, just saying that sometimes beauty can be dangerous. Have you ever seen a cancerous ovary up close?' he asked with a smile that, in the yellowish-red firelight, looked a bit sinister.

'Mohamed, why do we have to go through this each time? What happened last night?' She turned to me to explain. 'He does this — he brings his work home with him.'

'As if you don't. But I don't mind coming home and finding you at work,' he retorted, giving her a nudge. 'What I mean is, it is the most beautiful thing, and once you see it — to be able to see its beauty — it usually means it's too late,' he went on.

'What about cancerous balls?' The Diva joked.

He gestured at me. 'Imagine — you are a journalist, aren't you? — imagine a beautiful white cloud, covered by a reddish layer of needle-thin strings. And then, on top of that, the brightest rainbow stripes of blood red and brown all around it. In your hand, it's alive. Cancer — you know what cancer really is? It's your body trying to fight off something; you don't catch cancer like a cold; it's your body producing cells to protect the damaged ones. It's beautiful in many ways,' he said, sounding like a musician finding beauty in the pain that produced a song.

'Then why do we try to kill it before it kills us?' I asked him.

'Because we do not understand it. If you can't tell the difference between a friend and a deadly enemy from a distance, you can let them get closer. If it's a friend, then you are safe, but if it's your enemy, then he is within killing distance, and boom, you are gone. We do a pre-emptive strike. If it was your enemy, well, then I guess your gamble paid off. If it was a friend, your attack turns him into an even deadlier enemy. A recent study just showed this. It is like our war with Eritrea; it is the same thing — we couldn't tell whether they were friends or enemies, and we could not wait to find out. We went to war. It turned out they were our friend, whom we turned into a dangerous enemy. Cancer is beautiful in many ways,' he explained, but underneath his words, there was a real pain that I could not understand.

'What? You are a writer now, are you, Mohamed? Am I a cancer? Or is that what you wish on me now? You knew what I did before we met—'

'And yes, I knew. I knew you were beautiful, as you still are—'

'You know I am on the road again tomorrow — is this what this is all about? Poor Doctor Mohamed, at home with his two children while I sleep with strange men?'

She was tipsy and angry at the same time. Mohamed tensed up. Not for the last time I wondered why she had invited me into her home. We could have met in a hotel lobby or a coffee shop.

Then something seemed to click for her, and she groaned, raising the bottle to her lips.

'My God, it's not about me. Did something happen last night? How is the patient you went to see?' she asked him, passing the bottle to me and hugging him.

I knew I should have gone back to the house, but being what I am, I stayed, reasoning one of them would have asked for some privacy or walked off and come back when calmness had returned.

'She died,' he said. They hugged, making their world their own, leaving me, as one blues singer sang, on the outside looking in.

'And the baby, did it make it?' The Diva asked with so much empathy that I thought she would burst into tears.

'See, this is what I mean, Kidane — that was fucking six months ago. Both mother and child survived. I am talking about a different patient,' Mohamed said.

Kidane started laughing. It really was time to excuse myself. But then, Mohamed joined her and they laughed — I mean, laughing until they were down on the ground and rolling around. So much so that I was scared they were too helpless in their laughter to mind the fire. Leading two intense lives, they had to make it work, and they found catharsis wherever they could, I figured.

They both sighed and started laughing again. Astrophysics, medicine and the Tizita — I was either with two of the most dynamic, intelligent and sensitive human beings out in the hills and valleys of Ethiopia, or we were all very drunk. Either way, I was happy they had pulled me out of bed. The Diva, Kidane, in her red dress, flames lighting her unevenly, looking so beautiful, so present and in love — and alone at the same time — for that alone, it was worth it.

15

'Mohamed, can I ask you something,
since we are sharing the green?'

We sat around for a while, taking turns throwing dry brush
into the fire, taking delight as it flared up even higher. Kidane,
already drunk, still had enough sense to go to bed. There was
another bottle lying somewhere nearer to the fire. I looked
around until I found it, together with the glasses we had long
abandoned. The bottle was hot, and Mohamed let out a big
cheer, yelling that there was nothing like boiling whisky to
soothe the soul. He poured himself a long drink, looked over
at my glass, nodded and filled it to a point where I knew a spill
was inevitable. It reminded me of when I first met Kidane at
the ABC and her rather long pour, and I commented to him
that it must be a family trait.

'No, my friend, it's called the disease of plenty. The Americans
and their fast food, Kenyans and goat meat — diabetes and
gout. The disease of plenty for those who can afford it — it kills
us in the end.' He reached into his pocket and produced a
joint, lit it and said to me, 'But what better way to go, no? Now,
you take the green.'

I took a long drag.

'You see, Kidane does not like it when I smoke,' he explained as he impatiently beckoned I hand him the joint. 'Ethiopian versus Kenyan *Cannabis sativa*?' he asked.

A statistical tie we concluded.

'Ethiopian versus Kenyan runners?' I asked him

Another statistical tie, given our earlier sprint from the explosion.

'Ethiopian food versus Kenyan?' was his rejoinder.

We both laughed at the question.

'Cheers then!' he said happily.

'Cheers!'

'So, what do you need for Kidane's profile? I can only say nice things. I live here, you know,' he said with just a slight humour to his voice.

'Well, her music, what do you think of it?' I asked him.

He thought a moment. 'When my mother died, Kidane sang at her funeral. I laughed and cried at the same time, and people thought I had gone crazy. To this day, I do not know why.'

'Yes, it happens sometimes — trauma,' I offered.

'Yes, trauma. But I do not mean that kind of cry-laughter. I mean, I was laughing in pain and crying in joy at the same time. There is something about the way she sings the Tizita that brings out many full emotions at the same time. Or maybe it's because she is my wife. What do you think? You have heard her sing the Tizita?' he asked.

I thought back to the early evening Tizita-Malaika performance, and her 'failed' song at the ABC.

'That is what I am trying to figure out. That is why I am here. I want to understand...okay, I want to feel.'

'Remember the uncertainty principle — maybe we can never ever truly know,' he said.

'Mohamed, can I ask you something, since we are sharing the green? How does she live with herself? All that intensity, how come she does not burn up?' I said, thinking about what the old man had said.

He added more brush to the fire.

'This farm, her family — nothing can get her here — we all hold her together. You know you are the first journalist she has allowed here; I was surprised and angry, to tell you the truth. Do you know why she let you in?' he asked, leaning closer towards me.

'I have no idea. I was honest — I have a wound and scars.... I do not know where they came from.... I don't even know if they are mine.... Maybe she took pity on me. I need to find out more about her and the Tizita. I need to know — that is what I told her,' I replied, and asked him how they met.

It was the old man's son who brought them together 15 years ago. When he shot himself in the head, the old man found his body still twitching, probably death spasms, and thought he was still alive. He had sent for Mohamed. By the time Mohamed got there, Bekele was dead.

Mohamed and Bekele were age mates, but had never really developed a friendship. Mohamed was too much into books, and Bekele was more interested in sports, football especially. And he was good enough to be drafted into the under-16 national team. But, like his father before him against the Italians, when the call for freedom from Mengistu's tyranny came, Bekele signed up and distinguished himself as a guerrilla fighter. He could have written his ticket into almost any political office in the Meles Zenawi government, but he was a soldier's soldier, and in the new, blended army of former government and guerrilla fighters, he was named a major. And then the Ethiopian-Eritrean war — and he was once again killing his brothers with whom he had fought to get rid of their dictator. It was too much for him, Mohamed explained.

Did he know Kidane before then? Of course, he did. Everyone knew her as a talented singer. He had feelings for her even when they were kids. But she was the headmistress's daughter — only Bekele dared mess with her.

'She told me that the boys called her horse mouth?' I asked him.

'Boys can be stupid. What can they know of true beauty at that age?'

Something about his tone suggested to me that he was probably one of those boys. But that was fine by me. We are all allowed to rewrite our histories, as long as it was in meaningless ways. I do it all the time.

Bekele and Kidane's love affair was well known. It had started when they were very young, and Mohamed's first thought as he stood there, looking at the body, was that now he stood a chance with her. Bekele was buried; Kidane moved to the city, and it was not until two years later when she returned to bury her mother and look after her sick father that she and Mohamed reconnected again. And so had begun their courtship, until one day she asked him to kneel, and then she proposed.

'Love. Why didn't Bekele stay after the first war?' I asked him.

'If presented with the same opportunity as Bekele, what would you have done?' he shot back.

'It's not an opportunity—'

'You know what I mean,' he said emphatically.

'Probably nothing — my family was in bed with our dictator. I would have been on the side-lines at best,' I said, thinking that is exactly what I had done — stood on the side-lines as my friends joined the pro-democracy movements, showing off their eyes, bloodshot from teargas, like they were battle scars. Lives were lost, some through assassination and others torture, but my family and I, we thrived. My father would turn off the TV every time reports of the demonstrations came on and would shake his head from side to side, as if to say, *These youngsters have no idea what they are doing*. My brother had defended some of the arrested, but it was with the clinical detachment of a criminal defence attorney; innocence or guilt did not matter, just a question of whether he could get them off and get paid. And soon after, he re-applied himself to corporate law. But at least he had been in the fray — somewhat.

'Then we must not judge. He did what was right the first time, then the second time he thought he was defending what he had fought for the first time,' he said, more for me than for himself, I thought.

'You remind me of the brother I have but never really had,'

I said to him.

Jack never was one to pull me back; he would rather push me into whatever muck or raging waters were in front of me and then point a finger.

'You are wrong about that — your brother is always your brother,' he replied with conviction.

I did not say anything.

'Do you have children?' he asked.

'I like my freedom too much, so no. Why?' I asked in return, surprised.

'Believe me, I know they are not for everyone, but I cannot help feeling pity for those who do not. To not know absolute love — to give it and to receive it. I cannot help but pity that,' he said in a tone that was sad and passionate at the same time.

'I cannot miss something I do not know,' I said. I knew I sounded defensive but could not help it.

'I wake up in the morning, get the kids ready for school; sometimes Kidane is here; often she is not. Sometimes, when an emergency call comes, they have to do the best they can and stop at a neighbour's for breakfast on their walk to school. But I do — Kidane does — we do what we do because this community keeps us all alive. Can you understand that? No, you cannot, because you have nothing more to lose than yourself.' He was not being judgemental. He was reading me as much as I was reading him and his family.

I kept quiet.

'If I have learned one thing from the Tizita — it's precisely those things that we don't know that we miss; you just don't know it,' he said.

'Do you think people like me and you ever meet again?' he asked as an afterthought.

'Maybe. I hope so. But the truth is, we shall never meet like this again. It will always be in lesser circumstances. Another night like this? Very unlikely,' I answered, feeling both relieved and lucky.

'I...then a toast to a bigger fire. To the heavens!' he yelled at the sky.

He stood up, and I followed him to get a water hose. We sprayed the fire down to smouldering cinders.

* * *

Someone was knocking on my door urgently, and I ran to open it, half-asleep. Kidane walked in, opened my curtains. And as the sun streamed in, I realised she was wearing a tracksuit and muddied white running shoes. She rummaged through my bag as I tittered around in my boxers until she found shorts and a T-shirt, which she threw on my bed. It was 6:30 in the morning.

'Kidane, where are we going?' I asked her, the words finally finding their way through the fog.

'Don't you want to join me for a run? You will love it. It's a lot like Kenya,' she said. And in case I had any doubts that she was serious, she started jogging in place.

'I have no running shoes,' I protested.

She went out and came back with a pair of sneakers, her husband's, but they were too big for me. She stuffed two socks inside and handed them back to me. There was no way I was going to run in shoes stuffed with socks, so I put on my safari boots, knowing there would be some blisters coming my way.

We stepped outside to a beautiful morning; it must have rained sometime at night because the gravel path had small puddles of water, and the mist was thick and wet as the sun warmed its way through. These types of mornings — if you have lived in a rural area, you come to miss them. And given the right set of conditions, it is like a former smoker smelling cigarette smoke after a long time — it invokes vivid memories of comfort and welcome familiarity.

'I would rather not run,' I said to her. In fact, the last time I remembered running was during an all-high-school marathon try-out — 42 kilometres. Eight hours and countless scoops of glucose later, my friends and I staggered to the finish line. That was the end of my running career.

'No shame in resting, just like yesterday,' she teased.

And she was off — light, slightly bow-legged and smooth. I followed her. We ran for about 30 minutes. Whatever had been gripping my chest tighter with every exertion started to relax, but I knew I was running on pure adrenaline, and tomorrow morning, if not sooner, would be pure agony. I sprinted to catch up with her. Something I immediately regretted, as I felt the early tremors of a muscle pull. We stopped, and I doubled onto my knees.

'How long do you run for?' I asked her.

'About an hour,' she said.

'Why?' I asked, but that was not what I meant. 'I mean, you have a concert in a few hours. You will be exhausted,' I explained myself.

'Running — at that moment when I feel like I am almost dying — that is where the Tizita takes place for me. It gives me energy. That is how I know the Tizita is not about death, but about life,' she answered, now lying down so that her back was resting on the hill, her chest heaving.

I lay flat on the hill, feeling gravity tagging at my toes as the cool dew soaked in through my T-shirt. I tried to feel my feet through the heat of the safari boots and gave up. She undid her laces and laced up again.

'Can I ask you something? I have seen your posters all over the place. On YouTube you have millions of fans. You have been invited by presidents to sing in their palaces and you have declined. You are bigger than this place, this farm. What are you doing out here?' To take the edge off my question, I added, 'Is all this for your children?'

'It is home — this is where I grew up. This is where I get my music. For you, all you can see are hills and valleys, but for me, this landscape is like a living map of my life, of my history. I met a boy and fell in love here. I had my first period playing not far from here. My parents are buried here. These hills and valleys were once soaked with the blood of our freedom fighters. You see what I mean?' She stood up and started stretching.

"Hills and Valleys" by Buju Banton came to mind.

'When I am here, I have no nostalgia. Besides, why can't my singing also be like a city job, where every few months I get to go back home? Are you a city boy?' she asked.

'I grew up in an area much like this. I miss it. I miss it a lot actually, but I do not want to go back.'

I stood up and tried to stretch.

'Then for you, what you have is nostalgia and perhaps regret. For me out here, what I have is life, home,' she said in a tone that had a tinge of pity in it.

'Home? Home becomes the place we leave. That is how I grew up,' I said.

'What, are you crazy?' she asked, jabbing me on my shoulder with her elbow. 'Home, this place — here — this is what allows me to be in all the other places. Home is where you live, the place you always come back to, the place that sends you away to make money so you can come back.'

'The life of a musician — that is a day job for you then? Like a nine-to-five gig, or whatever the hours are?' I asked her.

'No, man. It is a life. Not a day job — it is also life,' she answered.

'But earlier you said—'

'I said that this is where I come home from my job. The musician in me might very well say the same about my being here, that this life is the job. Are you married?'

'No,' I answered, wondering why she was asking.

'Okay, let's say you, the tabloid journalist, the lover or the son — which of those lives is real?' she asked.

I did not answer.

'They are all real at different times, but the place where they are real at the same time is home. It is a sad life if you cannot have that,' she answered for me.

'And here, do they know you as The Diva? Do they know

you are The Diva?' I asked her, feeling less a journalist and more a person who had been wounded by a friend.

'So the gloves come off? I should not have run you too hard,' she said, a glint of humour returning to her face.

'No, that is not what I meant....'

'I am their child here, and my children are their children, and theirs mine — we live here. How can I be The Diva here? Why is that so hard to understand? The Diva, that is someone else's creation — not mine. But I am a musician — all the time — all the different mes are me here,' she said defensively.

'But you must want to be The Diva here, no?' I followed up.

'Are you rested now?' she asked, and before I could answer, she had sprinted off. 'See you at home!' she yelled.

I ran for a bit, gave up and started walking back. Running in safari boots was a terrible idea. The forming blisters were feeling like tiny waterbeds under my feet; I was in pain all over, thirsty, and the feeling of sweat drying on my face did not help. But I would not have traded that short conversation with Kidane. What I saw as contradictions, she saw as existence, as life itself. I now had a slight foothold in unfolding the enigma that was The Diva.

Except for several fleeting questions: was I falling in love with The Diva that did not exist or with the married Kidane? Was The Diva my fantasy or was it Kidane? I knew enough about telling stories — they were also about the storyteller.

16

'Come see the other me.'

By the time I made it back, Kidane was serving Mohamed and the kids hastily scrambled eggs. They had a good laugh at my expense. She went to the kitchen to toast some bread, only to curse so loudly that we all went quiet. Mohamed asked what the matter was, and she marched in and furiously placed a small loaf of bread with no crust on the table. Then I remembered Mohamed and me, high the night before, the munchies demanding something sweet, and the only thing we could find was bread. Mohamed had insisted he was going to make me the best peanut butter and jelly sandwich — it involved eating toasted crunchy crust. It was the best PB&J sandwich I had ever had, but we had not anticipated the fallout. The kids did not mind, though, so it balanced out in the end.

It was time to leave for the concert — the set up and rehearsals were going to eat up the rest of the day. The kids were also eager to play football with their father, so after quick, casual goodbyes, we were on our way. The same cab driver that dropped us off at the bottom of the hills was waiting for us at the end of the painful, long trek.

'Shall I stop at the other place?' he asked in English as soon as we got in.

'Yes,' she replied.

'What other place?' I asked her.

'You will see,' she answered, and they both laughed.

The cab driver's name I now learned was Mustafa, a Somali living in Addis. I guessed until he had seen you twice, he maintained his cover — xenophobia against Somali people any time the war in the Ogaden flared up was a constant fear. We spoke about xenophobia all over the continent — South Africa, Libya, Egypt; it seemed pan-Africanism was in spirit and not in practice. We talked about how the Islamic Court Unions might have done some good were it not for Ethiopia and the United States. And how Kenya had now finally invaded Somalia 'officially.'

The conversation moved on to the mundane — the cost of bread, petrol and so on, until we were back in Addis, where he drove to an expensive-looking building a few hundred yards from the African Union headquarters. I thought we were picking up someone, but we drove to the back, where he punched a few keys into a pad and large gates opened up to a garage. I asked Kidane again where we were going. She simply smiled.

Eventually we parked Mustafa's taxi next to a long Mercedes Benz that looked all the newer next to his Oldsmobile. We entered an elevator where he once again punched in a code, and we took the long ride up to the top floor to pick up someone I was now sure was a good friend, or Kidane's lover.

When it turned out he had the key to an immaculately furnished penthouse apartment and there was no one in, I started to suspect that they were lovers. They went to separate rooms. The suspense was killing my tabloid senses, so I started looking for clues — there were none. I looked at the magazines and newspapers on the glass coffee table. Before I could open the latest Ebony magazine with a barely dressed, hips-thrust-into-the-camera Beyoncé on its cover, Kidane, and shortly thereafter, Mustafa, returned.

Only it was not Mustafa and Kidane. It was The Diva and her bodyguard. The Diva came over to where I was standing frozen, mouth open, at once understanding what was before me and at the same time as confused as I had ever been. She was dressed in a long, white, tight evening gown, with a light shawl covered with the green, yellow and red of the Ethiopian flag wrapped around her bare shoulders, her long, muscular neck bare.

Mustafa was dressed in a tuxedo, and where before he had seemed thin and effeminate, even in his several-sizes-bigger shirts and trousers, the Mustafa that stood before me was a guy you did not want to mess with, his chest straining the shirt buttons as he adjusted a gun in his shoulder holster, put on his jacket and checked himself in the mirror to make sure that the gun was concealed. I recognised him — he was the man I had almost run into back at the ABC when I was leaving The Diva's dressing room.

'What is going on? I saw you at the ABC,' I said to him.

He shrugged and smiled.

'What's going on?' I asked The Diva.

She went over to the stack of magazines and newspapers, took one and threw it at me so that it fell by my feet. And that is when I saw *The National Inquisitor* headline: "Sex, Drugs and Rock-and-Roll Tizita" — the piece in which I had lied in order to bulldoze the money men at *The National Inquisitor* to send me to Ethiopia.

'You are not the only one with secrets. You are lucky I liked it,' she said with a laugh when I started trying to explain.

They walked to the door, and for a moment I thought they would leave me behind.

'Come,' she commanded, and I followed them, less a journalist and more like a boy caught lying. Mustafa flashed me a sympathetic, even friendly, smile.

What had I been thinking? And why was she letting me carry on? Whatever the case, I was going to give my readers a good story, regardless of the truth. I mean, had I written only about The Diva of Nairobi, would that have been the truth? Or if I wrote only about Kidane, wife and loving mother — would that be the truth? In a world of multiple covers and faces, only a fool would think the truth was the first face one saw. In journalism school, we used to have drunken debates in the same parties where I played my one Malaika song about objective reporting. Ever the radicals, we would agree there was nothing like objective reporting.

But we had it all wrong, because we placed the burden of objectivity on the journalists, who in turn bring their biases to the story, to be piled on by the biases of the editor, dictated by whatever corporation owned the paper. But we always assumed the subject of the reportage was objectively solid and stable. Well, what I was learning, or rather seeing, confirmed that both the journalist and the subject were in constant motion. And if both of you stopped and talked over a cup of coffee or a beer, that would be a sliver of the truth at that point in time. We had been applying the uncertainty principle to the wrong party.

The Addis Ababa Stadium and Millennium Hall — magnificence on steroids — displayed a country conscious of its image as the poster child of development. In many ways, the stadium itself was performing for the TV cameras, the blog writers and tweeters, because each story, whether it was about a football game, a political speech or music performance, had to begin with its vastness, filled with 60,000 people all there to watch, listen and commune. Sixty thousand people in one space produce electricity, current charged with anticipation, in the constant, loud, undecipherable murmur of talking and singing voices.

I had a choice to make, write it in the moment to help my readers see it as I saw it, or take notes and tell it to them as a story past. The energy...the magic of it all — it was not a word I had ever used before with my readers, but I loved them, so I wrote it as I was seeing it. I wanted them there with me.

Live! The Diva on Stage

The Diva is here to do a concert for soldiers, veterans, friends, family and anyone who cares to show up. It is free, so it's 60,000 people and probably another 5,000 standing outside the stadium, not to mention those watching from home. Backstage, The Diva standing there — surrounded by tech people, journalists, fans who had won backstage passes, The Diva surrounded by the machinery that produces the music we consume — looks so small, in danger of being crushed by all of it. She smiles, signs this, takes a photo, kisses someone on the cheek, shares a joke with an old friend. I look again — she is not in danger of being crushed by it all; she is in control, the skilful surfer who seems to be in danger of being swallowed by a massive wave but triumphs each time. Every now and then she looks at Mustafa, the leash that will keep her tied safely to her surfboard if the rising waters were to push her off.

The anticipation builds; the band, all men dressed in army jackets over khaki pants and army boots, are playing as if on a loop, repeating the phrase so that each time they return to the point where the musician should make an entrance, the crowd yells for The Diva. She calls me over — the waters respectfully part to let me through — and she whispers, 'Come see the other me.' She smiles at Mustafa, and he walks me over to a small VIP section and then hurries back. I can hear and feel the ocean of 60,000 people behind me. I am no longer a journalist — I am one of them.

I look around and see large-screen monitors set up all around the stadium showing her making her way to the front of the stage, Mustafa in front of her. Triumph, mixed with a self-conscious smile that suggests she knows how good she is, plays on her face. The Diva — no sign of Kidane anymore — walks onto the stage. The united horn section goes into high gear, the drums, bass and keyboards follow, and a storm of dancing song brews. She walks up and down the stage; she owns it. She stops every now and then, says something and playfully wags a finger at the crowd. I have no idea what the words mean, but I know enough now not to worry about what words mean but what her voice says — she is telling the men to be careful of her, or of others like her, or telling the women to be wary of men like the ones she is pointing at.

Call and response with the band, the horn section coming in slightly before she talks to the men — more like sings to them — with the band all quiet, and then as her voice gets angrier yet remaining playful, the band comes in. The drums set the tone — a few angry rat-a-tats as the horn section, the keyboards and The Diva remain silent — and then her, just her — her voice speaking to the 60,000 people comes in, magnified by the image of the beautiful, lone woman on stage, and we all go wild. The band comes in — and we are hungry for more.

She paces up and down stage, her voice whipping up the band into a frenzy — and then she does a simple gesture that almost causes a riot — the band comes to a stop, there is only silence. She runs to the centre of the stage and takes off her suit jacket, and then runs her fingers over the buttons of her white shirt, pretending to undo each one of them. The roar of a turned-on crowd; the band intervenes, but not before letting one of the trumpet players talk *to her, his trumpet approving, asking for more. It is simply the sexiest, most erotic performance I have ever witnessed, and I feel things in me stirring, made all the more intense by a turned-on, massive crowd. And then she moves on to a few more disco music-like tunes. We dance and dance; people sing along to her popular songs until their voices are hoarse. This is no Kidane on stage — this is The Diva, and I feel I understand her, even though I have no words to express this understanding. The Diva and her all-male band — she thrives, loves being in control of all of them, all their macho selves held and sewn together by her voice.*

Almost two hours into the concert, and a song ends. She bows her head and, lifting only her eyes so that it looks as if she is about to charge the crowd, she says, 'I believe in God.' I expect her to say she believes in the devil as well, but this is a different crowd — soldiers need no reminders of the devil. This group of men yet to be wounded or killed, yet knowing that for some of them, death is certain; and those who had survived and lost limb or faith, and the relatives of those who died — they all need hope.

The band leaves the stage in silence. Mustafa comes and hands me an envelope. 'She wants you to have this,' he says as he sits by me. A choir dressed in blue comes in, and standing in front of them is a krar player, short and overweight. I open the envelope — it's a Tizita. It's all written down by hand thanks to The Diva.

The krar starts off with a solo as The Diva sways from side to side, now more self-aware. She waits a little bit more and says something that Mustafa translates for me as 60,000 people get on their feet, yell, clap and shush each other. 'It's a Tizita by

Bezawork. She wants to pay homage to one of the greatest Tizita singers of all time,' he translates.

A few reps by the krar player. She closes her eyes and brings the microphone to her mouth, keeps swaying from side to side, as if waiting for a cue that only she knows. I remember this from her performance at the ABC. The krar player, fingers at times a blur, at other times picking up one note after the other, keeps nodding in her direction, as if telling her, I am waiting for you; enter now.

60,000 people still on their feet waiting, and the waiting itself feels like a song. The choir sways with her, waiting. The band members taking a break have also come out to the sides of the stage, a little worry and pride etched on their faces. And then, whatever she is waiting for, perhaps a perfect balance between the krar and the loud anticipation from the crowd, comes to pass. Her voice, hoarse from all the high-charged singing earlier, is cracked a bit, but it adds to the music. I finally allow myself to look at the lyrics. They are in Amharic, but I follow them, listening to her voice, not for words and their meaning, but as an instrument trying to tell us something. What does it matter what the words mean? I listen.

Hiiwot zora, TeQuma tizitan
Hiiwot zora, TeQuma tizitan
Dirron ayto madneQ, yesekenu eletta
Dirron ayto madneQ, yesekenu eletta
Deggun mastawesha, baynorewu tizita
Deggun mastawesha, baynorewu tizita
Negen baltemegnat, sewu
Negen baltemegnat, sewu...

*The cadence of her voice relaxes, the voice I know to be hers —
it's almost like she is having a chat with the Tizita. Her voice —
the word I have been looking for comes to me: her androgynous
voice — rising and falling with the bass and the krar, drawing out
sorrow as if from a well. And when she repeats 'Tizita, Tizita,' I
see split images of Bekele and her, alive and young and vital, the
tragedy of what awaits their happiness on the horizon. 'Love and
its mischief, it came and left,' her voice, the instrument, cries.*

Tizita bicha newu, yelib guadegna
Tizita bicha newu, yelib guadegna
Letamemech hiiwot, meTSnagna medagna
Letamemech hiiwot, meTSnagna medagna

*The way her voice quivers, life has become unbearable, cannot be
lived as is and something has to give.*

Eyayun malefun, lemedelign aynein
Eyayun malefun, lemedelign aynein
Eyayu malefun, lemedelign aynein

*What is she pleading for and whom is she imploring? Here I get
lost in my own thoughts. The Diva — I know she can hit any note
she wants. She did it with me just yesterday with her kids running
around the yard, the sun that had set just an hour before glowing
through the clouds. But this evening she is holding back, and
where her voice takes command and soars, she flicks her hand up
in the air as if to hold herself back, and she lets the krar play on
eight or so beats before coming back to the song.*

That gesture again, and I put the lyrics down. I start to watch each time she raises her hand — the gesture elides something. I watch hard enough to notice that she does that to pull herself back. The Corporal did it, the holding back, at the ABC, but not to the same effect as Kidane. We had been angry at his holding back because we wanted a bit of that flagellation that comes with facing one's demons — catharsis. But Kidane is getting rewarded — the crowd going crazy each time. The choir comes and completes the gesture by giving depth, as opposed to height, through a solo.

That gesture again! It hits me: the crowd is going crazy each time she holds back. It is so simple it makes me want to cry. The reason some preachers are better than others, or some poets better than others — they merely suggest, and your fears or wants, at their most absolute, manifest themselves. I can tell myself she is performing — but performance as I understand it is about show, fireworks — performances are not supposed to be what Kidane is doing, merely suggesting, being content to suggest and letting us do her work. I look at the lyrics.

Shimagilei Teffa, shibet ende'dirro
Shimagilei Teffa, shibet ende'dirro
Shimagilei Teffa, shibet ende'dirro
Shimagilei Teffa, shibet ende'dirro
Shimagilei Teffa, shibet ende'dirro
Shimagilei Teffa, shibet ende'dirro
Shimagilei Teffa, shibet ende'dirro

The choir comes in again, this time, allowing each voice to be soothing yet almost distinct. I can hear twenty voices, all of them with something to say, singing together — this loss, it's ours; it's not to be feared; it's to be embraced. It is in the loss that they find life; they play with their voices. And The Diva is somewhere in their voices; her voice strong and vulnerable, almost lost but at the same time carrying them all. And then they slow down and let the krar take the lead until it too slows down, and the song and performance end. The stage is rushed. I expect Mustafa to jump into action. He shrugs when I look at him.

'She is safest here — no one would dare touch her,' he says to me.

I look again. Her fans are not rushing the stage to take a piece of her, to take a memento home; they are hurling love and kisses at her. Others rush and stand at a respectful distance — they just want to be close to her. I ask him if he can translate as I ask the people who have overrun our little VIP section some questions, or rather, one question, What is the Tizita to you? I pick the people randomly.

A schoolboy still in uniform — It fills me with pride.

A soldier — It makes death feel warmer. *I ask him through Mustafa to explain a little bit more.* Death, we are all going to die — me, maybe in a war. The way she sings it? It makes me know I am part of life, and I will be remembered even after I am gone.

A couple that wouldn't be able to hide their love for each other even if they tried — If I was to lose her, I would kill myself, *the man says.*

And if he died, I would go on living — I would find the strength to live for the both of us, *she laughs, and they try to make their way to The Diva.*

An old white woman, high as a kite and dressed like a 1960s hippie — The Tizita is a mirror that does not like one single thing. *I ask her to explain, but she pinches me on my cheek playfully, as Miriam would do, and says,* Live long enough, son.

An old man with his son — My daughter died in the liberation war — I find comfort knowing I will join her soon.

The son/brother — The Tizita is the blood in our soil — the Tizita makes it boil. *I ask him to explain, and he says he has no words beyond that.*

Mustafa slaps me on my back. 'And you, my friend, what does the Tizita mean to you?'

I am taken aback by the question but also surprised by how readily the answer rolls down my tongue. 'Just how little of life I understand,' I answer. 'And you?' I ask him.

He looks over at The Diva, and I am almost afraid of what he will say. 'I will kill or die for her,' he answers.

17

*'By the way, you are wrong about me.
I am always me, even when I am many.'*

After the concert, The Diva was too wired to sleep, and some of her adrenalin rubbed off on me. Mustafa, perhaps because of chewing *khat,* was looking like he had just woken up. She suggested we go to an all-night juke joint. Juke joints immediately recall run-down establishments where black American plantation workers would get together for booze and music during the Jim Crow era. But they are universal, existing in translation across all cultures — speakeasies during Prohibition; shebeens in South Africa during apartheid; holes in the wall for those wanting to do modern-day slumming; and urban after-hour bars. Certainly, the ABC, or indeed the CRP, would have translated into a juke joint in Ethiopia, but with the twist of having a diversified economy.

Generally speaking, these holes in the wall tend to be in the most dangerous parts of a town, yet safety is all but guaranteed. And these islands of the great coming together under suspended reality have another thing in common: there is no being out of place — an alien straight from Mars could drop in and be served a beer without the bartender so much as showing surprise.

This juke joint, out in one of the less savoury parts of Addis, was aptly and ironically named Chivas Regal. The Diva (or Kidane), Mustafa the bodyguard (or taxi driver) and I, a journalist (or tabloid writer) were not overdressed — all of us were right at home with the white tourists; the trying-to-be-tough-looking teens from the neighbourhood; the drunks; those cheating on a spouse; and the various wealthy subsets of Addis. There was a house band, a guitarist, drummer, bassist and singer, doing Michael Jackson covers. The band recognised The Diva by dedicating "Pretty Young Thing" to her.

'The irony,' she quipped.

Some of the clientele also recognised The Diva, but not in the gushy American way of getting an autograph to sell on eBay. They instead bought a bottle of beer, glass of wine, whisky or one of the roses being sold by the universal resident cupid and had it brought to our table, waved a thank you from a distance before returning to their conversation. Every now and then, someone would come up to her and say something, touch her hand gently and then go back to what they were doing.

We worked our way through the wine, beer and knock-off Chivas fast enough to have caught up with everyone else inside of an hour. Mustafa, who in here most certainly did not have any work to do, was soon on the floor dancing to a cover of "Beat It."

'So, you have not said anything — how did I do?' The Diva asked me, half-jokingly.

'The truth?' I verified.

'Yes, your version of it anyway,' she answered.

'Am I talking to The Diva or Kidane?' I asked her.

'Ugh, how many times do I have to.... You are talking to me. All of us are me,' she answered, looking around as if bored, but I could tell I had just irritated her.

'I thought that you have an integrated multi-personality disorder — that is why you have two — perhaps more — lives, and many voices in one. I loved it,' I answered, after struggling for the right words.

She clapped her hands in delight. 'You know how to compliment a Pretty Young Thing,' she said with feigned sarcasm, or enthusiasm.

'The truth is, I pitied you,' I said.

She looked surprised.

'I mean, I pitied you because you cannot hear yourself and realise how great you are. You can never really surprise yourself. Something in you knows what you are going to do next. I wish you can experience yourself the way we just did out there,' I explained.

'See, this is why I brought you to Ethiopia. You think about this stuff even when you are wrong. Yes, a part of me knows what is coming next even when I improvise, but the feeling of it — that is the surprise. I do get to experience myself outside of myself — when I feel. I do surprise myself — that moment between knowing, feeling, then falling into an abyss. It is rare, I agree, but sometimes I do get to do things I wasn't supposed to do, even at the tip of it all.'

We both laughed seriously.

'At the concert, why didn't you hit the high notes? I know you can do it,' I asked, aware that I sounded like I was accusing her of a crime, like she had cheated the crowd.

'I think you know,' she said and tapped my forehead.

'No, I don't.'

'Yes, you do,' she countered.

'What do you mean?'

'Think back — was I the only one?' she asked, looking at me curiously.

'My writing?' I asked, feeling a sense of panic — I was in a space that was both utopia and dystopia.

'The journalist wants to be part of the story? No, nothing to do with you; that is not it.'

I thought back — she was right, the drummer would every now and then mute the drum with one hand while hitting it with the other; the saxophonists and trumpet players would every now and then threaten to take us on a soaring journey, only to come back to the fold. In other songs, she had done everything with her voice, as had the band with its instruments. And when, somewhere in the middle of the concert, she introduced each member, they had in turn showed off their chops. But not when playing the Tizita.

'Why?' I asked her.

'I told you before. Containment. The Tizita — it is private, a private love or sorrow that joins the public ocean of tears. We mourn and celebrate together and privately at the same time. A good Tizita walks that line — if you show off, you undo that balance. The people feel what they have lost, no need to slap them in the face with it. Besides, what can you tell an erupting volcano of the hotness of the lava? And the soldiers would never forgive me if I made them cry in front of each other,' she explained.

'They cried anyway,' I said to her.

She shrugged to say, *There goes that idea.*

'The worst Tizita is one that sounds precious. You know, like Whitney's "I Will Always Love You,"' she said, singing a bit of it mockingly.

There was one question I had been dying to ask, and now I had an opening. 'What do musicians like you — musicians who care about the craft itself, its beauty and fragility, and worry about its potential to harm and distance one from life itself — what do you think of your Hollywood counterparts?'

'Name the names,' she said.

'Madonna, for example. What do you think of her?'

She laughed. 'Madonna? How about Beyoncé? I would love to have her money — as a businesswoman. But the truth is, I don't think of them at all — as an artist, I don't,' she answered.

'But you are all musicians,' I said, regaining my balance.

'They entertain; they make people feel good or sad, I will grant them that — there is nothing wrong with that. But what I do.... Are you really asking the question I think you are asking?' she stopped and looked at me.

'I just...'

'Your Hollywood stars, they get on stage, and all they have is themselves, their voices, their aesthetic, you know, their coolness — me, and the others, we are motherfucking philosophers of the soul....' She stopped and looked at me when I started laughing.

'No, no — don't laugh,' she protested. 'Take your pop song — it's either sad or happy — it has no range. But the blues contain happiness and sorrow at the same time. A song with a single emotion? That is not music. A good song contains a rainbow of emotions. Children know this. When my daughter was a kid, she thought blues music had the colour blue. She would ask me, what is red music? What is white music? What is yellow music?'

'So then, what is the difference between the blues and the Tizita?'

'Is there a difference between languages? Between Swahili and Amharic?' she asked and then continued, 'Lots of difference, and yet there is no difference. In the end, we speak many languages to say the same things — see what I mean?'

I said no, and she shook her head and laughed.

'I guess journalists are not artists,' she said.

'You know, I have heard that the Tizita was first sung by wandering musician poets, then that it comes from singing the psalms — what is your version of the truth?' I asked her as she laughed.

'Yes, the truth of the Tizita has many versions. But I believe it comes from the language itself. Amharic is the Tizita in conversation. Or Tigrinya or Oromo — you know what I mean? We are the same people, no?' she asked, knowing very well I had no idea. She asked me for the lyrics she had given to me through Mustafa, and I laid them on the table.

'Listen to this: *Hiiwot zora zora, TeQuma tizitan / Dirron ayto madneQ, yesekenu eletta*. Listen carefully,' she said as she leaned into me and repeated the first two lines conversationally before singing them. I could hear it — the rhythm of the Tizita contained in the language, the soft *q* click adding a quick uptick to the syncopation.

'The other versions might be true, but the one truth is that without the rhythm of our languages, there would be no Tizita,' she said and playfully slapped the lyrics on the table.

'What do the lines mean?' I asked, hoping to get an English translation from her.

'*Without my Tizita, that sweet-sour memory / I can have no desire for tomorrow*,' she translated, then stood up to go join Mustafa on the dance floor. I got on my feet and joined them as the band did a jazz cover of "Thriller" — the crowd of misfits mimicking his zombie dance moves.

Speaking of Whitney, I wanted to dance with somebody — to connect, even drunkenly, fleetingly. There was a beautiful woman dancing. Just my luck, or more likely because she was on the dance floor, the band broke into their own Tizita, and I hesitated for just long enough for a white tourist to make his way to her.

'Fuck off. I am not going to share my Tizita. Just buzz off,' I overheard her tell the man, who, red-faced, walked away to the bar.

The woman glared at me, daring me to make the same ill-advised move. I was not brave enough. I looked over to see if

The Diva was watching, only to find her walking towards me smiling. She asked me if I wanted to dance.

'She just said the Tizita cannot be shared,' I said to her, pointing at the woman swaying by herself.

'She said that? There is a loophole — I sing the Tizita, I should know — we shall not be dancing to share — I will be teaching!'

We danced, my hands around her shoulders and hers on my hips — me feeling offbeat and lost, and she comfortably cupping my hips.

'The Tizita — if you hear a good Tizita, you want to hold your arms across your chest. The Tizita looks inwards,' she lectured.

'A mirror? It allows you to see yourself?' I asked, thinking of MJ's "Man in the Mirror" and how clichéd this was getting.

'A mirror — a reflection — gives you back who you are. No, the Tizita does more than that. It's more...refraction; every part of you refracts the other. A blindness of total, complete realisation: your arms, mirrors; your brain, a mirror; your heart, a mirror — and somehow, they are all talking to each other. A good Tizita folds you inside out and back in again,' the lecture continued.

'Jesus, sounds a bit violent,' I voiced out before I could stop myself.

'No, it's a beautiful thing to refract yourself back to yourself. Anyway, the point is, a good Tizita musician allows for that refraction. An excellent Tizita musician, no, wait...the once-in-a-lifetime Tizita musician allows for the refracted pieces to connect, to hear each other through their echoes. When you listen to a good Tizita, you can never be alone.'

She pulled me tighter towards her. In high heels, she was taller than I was. I leaned into her. For just a brief second, our slow dancing funnelled heat upwards through her dress, up her breasts and bra. I could tell she was as hungry as I was hard. I inhaled deeply. With each slow move and beat, I breathed in perfume, but not just hers; her desire, but not just hers; her breath spitting out alcohol, saliva, and her lips....

We pulled away even as we continued to dance close.

'How does it feel to perform for 60,000 people?' I tried to carry on.

'In front of 60,000, I am lost in them. But at a juke joint or the ABC, I can feel myself, each word, each note. I can see it in the eyes of the audience. We dance and sing together, you know?' she explained, pulling me towards her even tighter. I could feel myself becoming unbalanced — like I was falling into her, and it was both exciting and frightening.

'Kidane, what is it you want from me?' I blurted out.

'It's the other way around. I want you to learn something,' she said and pulled me against her as hard as she could.

'What?' I asked desperately.

'Not every desire has to be met,' she said and walked away before the song came to an end.

I had to think fast how to solve the little matter of my tent. For cover, I coughed violently, bent downwards and walked back to the table. Had I lost her? No, wait, in all honesty she was never mine to lose. It felt more like something had snapped

— for better if the sexual tension was behind us now, or for worse if that was the only thing holding us together. At the table, we continued on as if nothing had happened. Nothing had happened.

By 3 or 4am, the juke joint band was just jamming, throwing each other notes here and there until the bass finally caught a hypnotic puttering rhythm. The drums were just steady, with the guitar coming to life every now and then to give reggae-accented slaps to the rhythm. The singer, quite drunk, was at the counter trying to talk up the woman who had told off the white tourist, and they seemed to be getting along. The Diva walked to the microphone and started humming. The bass — lazy, hypnotic, puttering here and chugging — and she singing along, humming, throwing a word here and there, sometimes yodelling, showing off her voice in ways she had not at the concert.

The band played on and on until the song was no longer something outside of us, until it became so much part of our life, that life at the juke joint resumed: stories between friends, laughter, sounds of a breaking bottle — the nothings that make most of our evenings and nights. The song became the very air we were breathing. And at the same time, it was breath that announced itself, that reminded us of pain and love at the same time, extremes of several emotions felt at the same time. The band played on and she sang on, at some point taking a break to go to the ladies' restroom. When she came back, the bass player went to the bar to get a beer, and the drummer took a puff of one thing or the other. They played and lived, and I guess we listened and lived.

Close to dawn, we heard loud knocks on the door. It turned out the juke joint was a restaurant by day, and it was time for us to leave.

Mustafa drove me back to the hotel. I was sitting up front, and The Diva in the back. We drove in silence, no music except the hum of the Benz. When we arrived at my hotel, she called out to me as soon as I stepped outside, and I went to her window expectantly.

'So, you are going to see The Taliban Man next?'

'Yes, in a few hours, after a quick nap.'

'Tell him I am trying to bring him in.'

She asked me to get closer, and I leaned in. She kissed me on the forehead.

'Into what?' I asked her.

'Just tell him that. By the way, you are wrong about me. I am always me, even when I am many. See you in Nairobi,' she said as they drove off.

For a moment, I wanted to run after them just to catch a last glimpse of her. She was the most charismatic, magnetic, beautiful, kind and cruel person I had met so far in all my journalistic travels. Who she was? My problem. The Diva, Kidane, superstar, mother, wife, businesswoman — she was always herself by one or all of her names. The same person, but living in a world that demanded she divide herself to be herself. And she, as an army would, activated and deployed all her selves so that she lived out a full life — Mohamed, her kids, her fans — me, her confessor — is that why I was here with a front row seat? To reconcile all of her selves in one single narrative that would go out to the world? A record of her many selves reconciled into one story?

But even as I was trying to work my way through the fog, lines for my *National Inquisitor* profile were forming — first sentences, all of them trying to prepare my reader:

For The Diva, a song is many people — too damn poetic.

Many voices sing one song — uninteresting and missing the point of who she is.

A one-song orgy — that might just do it, but already a mixed metaphor, there was nowhere to take it. I needed an opening line that would allow the rest of the story to spill out easily.

To sing the ultimate Tizita, one that taps into our collective subconsciousness, The Diva has disintegrated into several fully formed personalities. When she sings, her voice is a chorus — too damn long.

Kidane, aka the double-edged Diva, is a chorus unto herself — almost there. I had to keep working on it.

18

The Taliban Man

'For some people, sanity and insanity are truly a choice.'

I was sitting in the music room of the Progressive International High School in Addis waiting for The Taliban Man's former music teacher. It felt much easier to make my way through JFK Airport security than to get a guest pass to go through the PIHS security, but soon I was passing immaculately groomed and uniformed boys and girls, walking about and talking in hushed, respectful tones, on my way to the classroom where I would meet with Mrs. Hughes.

I could have been back in my high school in Kenya — pristine, disciplined, green, rich — elite. Even the way the students walked with the confidence of knowing that the future and the country were theirs for the taking reminded me of my friends in high school. Though, looking back now, I wonder if the confidence also masked the pain of knowing our rich and powerful parents were part of the problem — that they were rich because others were poor. It was not something we talked about, but the silence that followed a news report that so-and-so had been disappeared or detained, or millions of shillings were missing from one ministry or the other said quite a bit.

How does it feel to go through life knowing you are part of the problem? And how do you go about living knowing you are part of the problem? Two different questions. You compartmentalise and hang out only with others like you. And you have ostentatious, loud fun and crash an expensive car or two.

Mrs. Hughes walked in. She had long, silver dreadlocks, and her nails were painted in Rastafarian colours — a 65-year-old ball of energy. I did not ask her how she was allowed to teach at such a school, but I would think her whiteness came with the privilege of looking and dressing however she wanted. But it still said something about her — she must be damn good.

'Why is a fucking tabloid in Nairobi interested in my Yosef Kabede?' she asked as she showed me to a student chair.

I explained the competition and how *The National Inquisitor* is the most read newspaper of any kind in Kenya and that it would be good for The Taliban Man's career.

'Of course it will. I can't imagine a better person for a tabloid than Yosef, The Taliban Man,' she said and slapped her knee, laughing.

'Sometimes, our stories are picked up by international tabloids as well — and I intend on telling a good story,' I added.

'There can never be a genuine Tizita competition. How can one judge a Tizita? I mean, have you found a way of weighing a soul? Anubis, where is thy feather?' she asked.

'Anubis?'

'An Egyptian god. To get to heaven, your heart has to be

lighter than a feather. Anubis does the weighing. You cannot judge a Tizita unless you are Anubis,' she explained with schoolteacher patience. 'What is happening over there in Nairobi is simply obscene,' she added, with mounting anger.

I could understand why it would seem that way to her, and for most Ethiopians, I assumed. It was tantamount to taking something dear to a people and lampooning it. But she had not seen what I had seen, and I tried to explain it to her: how the musicians were in control, how they each got on stage and gave us something different and how, in the end, they had performed together.

'Surely Anubis must know that while there are souls that weigh the same, no soul is the same?' I asked her. 'The Tizita won that night,' I added before she could answer.

'Well, I am glad that is all happening at an off-shore site,' she said sarcastically.

She started to say something else then changed her mind. 'Here, let me show you something instead.' She walked to an upright piano. She played a minute or two of a complicated classical song. She was impressive; the music room temporarily transformed into a concert hall.

'That piece — do you know it?' she asked.

'I do not. I only know bits of Beethoven — that's about it,' I answered truthfully.

'Not all classical music is by Beethoven,' she said with a laugh. 'That is one of the hardest songs to master; technically very difficult, the feeling to capture it and play at the same time, almost impossible. You either play it — or you feel it. But at sixteen, Yosef had mastered it. I have known only one other person to do it as well, his sister. She was almost as good as he was...,' she said, looking up at me, waiting for me to ask the inevitable question.

'What happened to her? His sister?'

'Lawyer — a fucking lawyer — a lawyer joke!' she spat out.

'Why did she choose law over music, do you know?' I asked her.

'For some people, sanity and insanity are truly a choice,' she answered.

'Mrs. Hughes, Yosef and hip-hop — what do you think about that?'

'You want me to say it's a waste, don't you? No, it's brilliant; different forms of music, they need to speak to each other. His talent is so massive — if anyone can do it, he can. He does not know it, but he is my little messiah,' she said with a wistful smile on her face, instinctively running her hands over the piano keys.

Her music students started trickling in.

'Mrs. Hughes, that piece you just played, who is it by?'

'Maurice Ravel, *Gaspard de la Nuit*. But even your Beethoven — they could do his toughest pieces — youth and genius....'

The way she said, 'youth and genius' — all teachers must have a student they regret.

Later I would look into Ravel's piece, its emotional range, from intricate to dangerous — at 16 years, I would never have listened to that, let alone want to play it. But The Taliban Man and his sister, they both grew up taking what they had for granted.

'Is it that he feels he cannot own classical music? It can never be his?' I asked, and she looked at me, surprised.

'Do you own life, yet others have lived and continue their lives? In classical music, you own what you play; there is no ownership. It's like life — you own the life you live, yet others have lived before you, and billions live alongside you,' she answered.

She looked straight at me. 'Only I know what I have unleashed into the world. Give Yosef my love when you see him. You are going to see him, aren't you?'

As she walked me to the door, she said, 'Mind your head.' I was nowhere near tall enough to hit the doorway, so I turned and looked at her.

'Mind your head,' she said again.

19

_'If you have ever in life wished to be in
with the cool kids, this is it.'_

In contrast to Kidane's modest home in the hills on the outskirts
of Addis and The Diva's not-so-humble apartment in the city,
The Taliban Man lived in an enclave of wealth carved out of
a well-to-do suburb. In this enclave, the houses — with armed
guards at the massive gates, which opened up to winding roads
paved with marble and other shiny stones — were monstrous.
Once, in a suburb in Harare, I saw a massive house built to
look like a yacht, but it was an anomaly. Here, I am talking
about a suburb so extreme that it would seem this was where
extravagance came to shop.

I was observing all this sitting in the back of a bright red
limousine that I knew to belong to The Taliban Man because
the plates yelled TM. When the lobby had rung to tell me that
my ride was here, I walked outside to find the bellboys pointing
at the bright red limo. Where before, the bellboys simply did
not see me, they now rushed to open the doors. I, of course,
hoped that word was going to spread that I was someone who
knew somebody and could be a VIP myself.

I felt good being in the limo, and I rolled down the partition to chat with the driver who, as it turned out, spoke very poor English, but at least I could share my excitement by asking him a few questions, like how long he had worked for The Taliban Man and what kind of a person he was.

'He is a simple man. And also very, very, very — how do we say? — very privacy,' he answered and rolled up the partition before I could ask another question. Style and attitude even in those who worked for him — I liked him already. He was my kind of subject: flashy and perfect for my readers.

We finally drove up to a gate with a huge, neon-lit guitar hanging above it. We waited for the guards to call someone in the house, and gates rolled open, the hum of electricity making it feel like it took longer than it actually did. Dinner was starting at 6pm. I looked at my watch, it was 5.55 pm — right on time. The driver opened the door for me and, stepping onto the marble driveway, I immediately felt underdressed, like I should have been wearing a formal suit, or if not, a bohemian-ish torn jeans outfit that spoke the language of careless money. My corduroys, my fucking safari boots with my still-blistered-but-now-manageable feet and a jean jacket were out of place above the marble. I gave myself a pep talk to remind myself that I too came from wealth and power. *Hey, you might even be the president's son,* I told myself.

Eight or so limos pulled up, and young people, mostly in their twenties and thirties, stepped out wearing expensive-looking skinny jeans and various forms of Nike sneakers. Obviously, they knew each other, and they hugged and chit-chatted as I, the older gentleman in my late thirties, stood alone there with my little reporter kit. The Taliban Man stepped out of the house and walked into the driveway dressed in a long, dashiki-looking shirt over white pants and sandals, and a colourful *gabi*, the long scarf wrapped around his shoulders. Servers dressed in black suits and skirts carrying champagne bottles and glasses followed him. He appeared a bit high, or tipsy — or most probably both.

'Welcome!' He kissed his right fist and pointed to the sky. We introduced ourselves in the driveway; some of his guests had variations of his name without the ease of his — Sandinista Man, Cubano Man and so on.

He walked over to me and put his hand around my shoulder.

'And this is the reporter,' he announced.

'How about we call him the Repo-Man?' someone yelled, to laughter. For the rest of the evening, I was known as Repo-Man.

The Taliban Man showed us around the house, though it really was for my benefit. His house is the closest I have been to a house in Rome as I imagine it. There were chiselled statues, only this time, instead of being Michelangelo's *David, Bacchus* and *Angel*, they were recognisably African heroes — Shaka Zulu, Bob Marley, Miriam Makeba, Steve Biko and others. In the huge, dome-shaped sitting room, my eyes followed pencil-thin lights that shone on the Sistine chapel painting, only instead of a white God giving a jolt of life to a wilting Adam, it was Menelik giving life to Che Guevara shortly after his execution in Bolivia.

We made our way through the mansion to the backyard, where there was a band playing some jazz standards by a massive pool. There were several grills sizzling with all sorts of goodies, and three bar stations with expensive beers and liquors. At the bar, inspired by the Chivas juke joint The Diva and I had patronised, I asked for a glass of Chivas as I debated how I was going to be a journalist when all I wanted was to be part of the crew and have some fun. The word camouflage naturally came to mind; I would meld in with the crowd and party — an observer-participant. After all, the Repo-Man is in the house!

The Taliban Man — I had done enough research of his background to know that he came from a wealthy family. Not just the wealthy, the powerful wealthy, two or three degrees removed from the president. But, unlike my parents, who liked to keep simple and dull, his family was part of the new cosmopolitan Ethiopia. A father in his fifties educated at Harvard, a PhD in economics, and a white English mother, an MIT-educated astrophysicist who loved the 'absolutely dark Ethiopian night,' as a newspaper write-up had quoted her as saying. They were now on various advisory boards and consulted for firms trying to set up shop in Ethiopia. His mother, though, was still researching, writing and giving conference papers.

His parents were out of the country, somewhere in Singapore on holiday. Going on a holiday, now that is something my parents would never dare do — they might have to talk to each other. I was disappointed I would not get to see The Taliban

Man's parents in person, but they had agreed to a Skype conversation. They might as well have given me a press release statement saying they loved their son very much and supported him in all his endeavours, because that was pretty much all I could get out of them. What did they think about his music? They thought highly of it. And his decision to give up classical music for hip-hop? They had brought him up to do the right thing for himself, and they were sure that he knew what he was doing. They kept looking at what I figured was a clock on the wall, and it seemed best to let them go.

'Tell our son we shall see him in a day or two,' they said, and that was that.

The Taliban Man's friends reflected his dynamism, and I was pulled right in. They knew themselves as part of the new Ethiopia — young lawyers, university professors, TV and radio broadcasters, bloggers with large followings, musicians and dancers, Silicon Valley types now venture capitalists, and returnees. Yes, as in Kenya, the old corrupt guard was after their souls. And what they offered — easy money and power in return for their consciences — was tempting enough, but there was something about their easy confidence that made me hold out hope. In time — and by that I mean in five or so years — the die would be cast, and perhaps they would have fulfilled their destiny of becoming part of the problem, but for now, out of this outstanding group of young people, two stood taller: Binyam, his friend, and Maaza, The Taliban Man's sister.

Binyam had made his money on Wall Street and returned

to Ethiopia to be part of the team building the Addis Stock Exchange from the ground up. Coming back after the stupidity and violence of Mengistu, Binyam had fit right into Zenawi's Ethiopia, an Ethiopia eager to build skyscraper cities with the hope that glitter and gold would trickle down into the poor urban and rural areas. Young and handsome, armed with the easy confidence or even righteousness of being part of something bigger than himself, he literally embodied a man of his times.

But not so much Maaza, a lawyer by training who had made partner in a law firm in New York, but had instead followed the dream of building the new Ethiopia. Unlike Binyam, who had set up shop in the business centre, she had set up a law office smack in the middle of Addis Ketema, Ethiopia's equivalent of Nairobi's River Road, a poorer sibling of the business world, where one found the small traders of second-hand clothes, cheap radios and TV's, and curio shops. These were the areas outside the protection of global capitalism laws, and police raids to shut down illegal kiosks and traders without licences were the norm. And so she was often in court defending or suing on behalf of the struggling small traders. She knew full well that Ethiopia had as yet to turn its back on the unforgivingly brutal and corrupt crony capitalism of the old. But just looking at her, beautiful and expensively dressed, with her peers in The Taliban Man's mansion, there was no way of knowing all this. I was to learn bits and pieces of their lives as the night wore on.

As I walk you through the night, imagine this group of dynamic young men and women at a party — they have earned the right to be here and to have a good time. Some are in the swimming pool, others huddled together talking politics, poetry and philosophy; lovers are holding hands and kissing, others awkwardly trying to make conversation to get laid for the night; others are quite drunk and are dancing by themselves. Imagine the band every now and then playing a crowd favourite that brings all the partiers together, like the Electric Boogie, and all of us, some in bathing suits and dripping wet, doing the synchronised electric slide.

Let me put it another way, if you have ever in life wished to be in with the cool kids, this is it — only they are also doing serious and rewarding, if not necessarily good, work. And they are here to have a good time.

20

'It freed my talent and me —
I refuse the pressure of making history.'

It is close to midnight when The Taliban Man goes to the mic and without any introduction launches into a beautiful, intensely personal poem. The poem on this night comes from a place of pain, of abuse and cold love, yet the child has grown up, gone through the pain and is now ready to embrace and be embraced. I will look it up later — it's called "Poem at Thirty" by Sonia Sanchez. He repeats the first line: 'It is midnight, no magical bewitching hour for me' and picks up his guitar. He starts rapping to heavy rock-and-roll chords. He says he has been trying to have more fun with his music and gets to it.

I am The Taliban Man!
I am the Caliban Man, against which all breaks
Them drone missiles drill our oil and blood
And them over there mining our pain for their gain
And we mine and mime back saying, give us this day
Our daily bullets, we have a brother to kill we have a sister
to kill

The Caliban Man will IED you every time you ask him for
his ID
My DNA is not for sale to the highest bidder. Your drones
want to send
Me to heaven in pieces, but my IED says I will send you to
hell in two pieces. Do
Not sell me your dirty bullets telling me I have a sister to kill,
I will not do your bidding, I will not be sold to the highest
bidder!

The Taliban Man is here to stay
Here to say, I am the rock-man
Against which all breaks,
Strike a child, you strike the Caliban Man
Strike my bitch and you have struck the rock-man

Give me your George Bush, so I can scatter, scatter him
In the bushes, I will return your emperor and your dictator
Give us back our Obama and we will teach him the African
Way of peace, but if you don't, The Taliban Man
Will IED him back to Kenya-land!

Why don't you man up and give me your hungry for justice,
Live up to your bible and give me your hungry for bread,
Yes, the Caliban Man knows of your long welfare lines
I will tell you what - I am The Taliban Man and my name is
your
Bane!

The Taliban Man is here to stay
Caliban Man here to say, I am the rock-man
Against which all breaks,
Strike a child, you strike The Taliban Man
Strike my bitch and you have struck the Caliban Man.

He is having fun, and his laughter is joined by that of his friends as the house band joins him back on stage, and they keep playing as other guests come on stage and pick up an instrument or sing.

What follows I can only describe as hours of an orgy of creativity — dirty, raw, personal, intense — an orgy that creates as much hunger as it satisfies, as musician after musician takes the stage. The set-up is like that of an open mic, but not exactly. There is no order, no one looking at the watch. Whoever is on stage plays or sings until they are done, and then just as gracefully (or as drunkenly and as ungracefully) as they had entered the stage, they exit to applause. The Taliban Man's stage is a place where the music is as true as speech, as true as a conversation with all its starts and hiccups and silences as one searches for meaning, or the right words.

Well, some of it is bad and 'jars my drink lobes,' as one of Soyinka's characters famously quipped — or, to put it in more contemporary terms, seriously fucks up my high. The krar, played by one of The Taliban Man's friends, ends up sounding too busy when it goes up against the hired house band — like the showmanship of an amateur boxer in the ring with a Mayweather in an exhibition match. Others shut down the band

and do karaoke with their iPhones and iPods held against one of the mics, their voices out of key, screaming out the song they are streaming.

But out of this stream of partier-performers, Maaza stands out. It is the house musicians and The Taliban Man who call her to the stage. Underneath the yells of encouragement, I can feel everyone is taking her just a little bit more seriously. She gets on stage and playfully shoos the piano man away. The drummer does a solo and then the familiar rat-a-tat, rat-a-tat before coming back down to the slow beat of the Tizita. The rest of the musicians join in with what they know, each wanting to leave their own mark on this Tizita. So we end up with a bit of jazz, classical music and Lingala, all on the rail tracks of the Tizita. It does not work. Classical guitar — fleeting and heavy, intricate and yet violent — its schizophrenia cannot be contained within the form of the Tizita. The jazz is also fighting the form imposed by the Tizita. The jazz is getting lost inside the Tizita — and at other times, it makes the Tizita formless, like when The Taliban Man's jazz guitar, with its in-between clean chords, announces itself and makes a break, only for it to be put in check by Maaza's piano. The more they struggle, the more the Tizita pulls them back, and the more they sound discordant. They come to a stop in a jumbled heap. Silence follows.

Maaza tears into Beethoven's Fifth Symphony with such ferocity that I can feel the casual party fun draining away. We crowd around the stage. The band members leave their instruments and stand around her. Only The Taliban Man remains, with his hands on the guitar strings to mute it, eyes closed, facing her direction, *as if to receive the violence on his naked face. She hammers the pompousness out of us — and then again. One more time, she rips the skins right off our bodies. She cheekily runs tender tendrils along our raw skins and prances away, skipping, thrilled — and now needing her, we trail after her.*

Again, she thunders, but this time The Taliban Man joins her, and he picks at the Fifth Symphony alongside her, as if competing to see who can express the widest range of emotions, complete on their own, but tenuously held together by a fragile thread. They throw tantrums; they take leisurely walks; vicious past fights and tensions are brought up, long forgotten familial wars. And being the exhibitionists that they are, they stray from the song and their conversation to tell us of past loves, and they giggle in embarrassment and laugh, all in the piano and guitar. And then their individual stories run their course, and they tell us about war and peace and the in-between tensions of war without cause and peace without meaning — then they start playing together in such harmony that the violence in their playing becomes peaceful and soothing.

By the time they are done, the realisation that the party has lost its lustre, that it cannot compete with the intensity that they have just displayed, hits us all. It is an excellent performance, too good for the kind of party where it is release we seek. And it feels like there is nowhere else to go but back home and, in my case, back to the hotel.

Not so fast, though. The Taliban Man says something in Amharic, laughter ensues, and as Maaza leaves the stage to applause, two groups of roughly ten people each get on stage, the men on one side, the women on the other. The band starts playing what I recognise as an Ethiopian traditional song. The men sing one verse and the women reply, but there is so much laughter, some people close to tears, others rolling on the wet marble by the pool, that I seek out Maaza, congratulate her and ask her what is going on. It turns out the revellers have taken a revered traditional song and turned it into a dirty song. The call and response — men bragging about how they were going to fuck the women with dicks that were so long that they had to be tethered to their ankles, and the women replying and saying that what the men really wanted was for the women to fuck them in the ass with their clits and strap-ons. The song goes on like that —machismo and hyper-masculine metaphors of cannons and fucking, and the women cutting the men back to smaller sizes.

This is, of course, not peculiar to this group of young men and women. We do the same thing in Kenya, where we take a popular song and subvert it. For example, "Malaika," the love song, becomes one of longing to fuck but the result is blue balls. Kenny Rogers' "Coward of the County" late at night becomes "Booty of the County." There is the all-time Kikuyu late-night favourite, a love song where the man is leaving late at night to go to work, or to war or someplace, and he is telling his girlfriend to close the door, but not to bolt it, as he will be back soon. The late-night drunken choir would turn it into a plea that she put her underwear back on, but not all the way; morning will not come before he gets another hard on. The sexualised mock performance ends, and the party, reenergised, resumes with new purpose.

* * *

'So, your brother, what do you think?' I asked Maaza. I did not let on that I wanted to find out from her why she never pursued something which, to us sitting on the outside, was a visceral talent.

'His music, what do you think?' I rephrased.

'I will give you two answers, one for you and the other for your paper — deal?' she answered, and I nodded in agreement.

'He has not found his way yet, but when he does, the world better watch out — that is for you. And this is what I want him to read in your paper, your tabloid, I mean. Quote me as saying he needs to be himself, to find the music he was meant to play. He needs to be himself. Quote me directly here — he does not need to wear his pants low.'

'You have a problem with hip-hop?' I asked.

'No, but it's not what he is meant to play,' she answered plainly.

'What is he meant to play? Ethiopian music? Classical? Jazz?' I asked.

'Only he knows, and he does not know it yet. It's like Fela Kuti — when he was in the United States playing jazz, no one could have predicted what he would play in a few years. Even he himself did not know, but he became himself, and all the parts fused in him, and he produced a sound like no other. That is Yosef's future.'

'I met with Mrs. Hughes today...,' I said, to her sigh.

'I am so tired of this bullshit! You know, you can be good at something, even excellent — hell, even talented — but it does not mean that is what you want to do. I did not want to be hauling ass and piano from concert to practice, playing to stiff audiences. I love people — I am doing what I love.' Her voice was somewhere between anger, pain and irritation.

Later, when I ask The Taliban Man about Maaza, he will tell me she should have been a musician — that was her calling, but she was the casualty of their parents wanting her to make something of herself. The same answer Mrs. Hughes had hinted at. But as it turns out, she knew, or might know, herself better, and she became a poor people's lawyer, still servicing and freeing souls in the courtroom.

'And how did you escape the same fate?' I will ask The Taliban Man.

'I am doing what I need to do. I fought back,' he will say, but I cannot help but feel that Mrs. Hughes would have added that he fought back by going overboard.

I could feel the loss that Mrs. Hughes must have felt knowing that, even as we spoke, Maaza could step into any concert hall and hold her own, and with practice, win a coveted spot in the world of music. I am the wrong person to judge, however, being sure my professors back at BU were probably saying the same thing about me — the African who could have broken into the ranks of *New York Times*, CNN and the likes. Certainly, that is the dream my parents had for me when I went the way of journalism. It could be said that tabloid journalism was my way of excessive fighting back. And the answer I would give would be very much like The Taliban Man's — I am doing what I see I need to do.

Maaza stood up to get a fresh drink, but I sensed she wanted to get away from me. I made my way to the hot tub, where a couple was having a heated conversation, so I listened in.

'We imagine God as an absolute, but what if God, with all that power, absolute power all round, turned out to be as whiny as we are? For fucks sake, give God a six-string guitar that is out of tune — tell him, *Hey, Mr. God, no using powers, just jam your butt off.* Then put God next to Jimi; say to him, *Jimi, show the good Lord what you can do.* Who do you think would win?' the young woman was asking her boyfriend.

'Jimi would take it home,' the man said, to their laughter.

'Yeah, possible — but this is what I think — I think Jimi would want God to win. 'Cos if you think you are better than an absolute something, what else is there?' she countered. 'Don't you then take his place? And what is fun? To be all powerful is to be amorphous — no limits — you are just there, spilling out of bounds all the time.'

'But here is the better question, would God allow Jimi to cheat in order to save face, or would he accept defeat? Would he say that the Jimi I created is a better guitarist than I, his creator?' the man asked playfully.

'Hell, no — they both need each other — that is the point I have been trying to make,' she replied.

Before they could continue, The Taliban Man joined us in the tub.

'So, what do you think, eh? Not a bad party,' he said as he slipped off his sandals and put his feet in. 'Time to make some toe soup — motherfucking tasty, no?' he added, to the laughter of the couple who jumped out of the tub in pretend disgust.

'It's certainly a great party — so much talent around you,' I replied.

'No, I am asking you what you really think,' he said, shaking his head from side to side.

'I like it here. Your parents, what do they think of your music?' I asked.

'Shit man, they don't give a shit. If I am not all classical, I embarrass them. I have some success but nothing major. I need an album out there, something that will do well.'

'So who pays for all this?' I asked him.

'Who do you think?'

'Yeah, when I spoke to them, they said they supported you....'

'I am a cliché — rich parents throwing money at their kids instead of.... They wouldn't even see you, and they live, like, a few houses from here.'

'I thought they were out of...I thought they were busy.' No need to add to their personal issues their lie that had no real consequence to my story.

'Is that really what you want to know? Who pays for my shit? Like, you came all this way for that?' he asked, genuinely disturbed at the thought — maybe even a little disappointed.

'No, you are right. I came for more than that. I am searching for something I cannot name yet — something buried deep in the music,' I answered.

'No, brother, you are looking for something buried deep in you,' he said and laughed.

'Perhaps. It would be easier if we can all rip into our chests and peer in,' I replied.

'That is what music is for, to find your secret,' he replied, aware of how wise he sounded.

I took out my notebook and read to him what Maaza had said.

'Hell, man, you're cutting deep; that is my sister. Come with me. Let me show you something. You better bring something to drink — you will need it.' He sounded resolute.

I grabbed the nearest bottle of Chivas floating in the pool and followed him. We walked towards the fence, where there was a guard standing by a much smaller gate, which he opened with a smile. The Taliban Man reached into his wallet and gave him some money with a slight bow. It was something I had been seeing over and over again, so I asked him about it.

"He is older than me. Unlike Kenyans, who throw money at waiters, here we are first and foremost all human beings," he answered.

'That is true, but you are still you, and he is a watchman,' I pointed out.

'That is true also, but why abuse someone's dignity?' he replied gently.

We stepped onto a paved path lit with floor lamps. We walked for about ten minutes and then came to a forested area. He found a long stick and beat the bushes until they opened up to a path overgrown with grass, and we kept walking. A small hill and at the top looking down, there was a graveyard. It was still, save for the noise from the party, faint laughter and music in the background. I could see the shimmer of a stream that was somehow not running, dead leaves and small branches floating, doing a slow dance to nowhere. A small bridge, and we crossed into the graveyard and darkness.

We took out our mobiles and used their flashlights to read the names on the headstones as he pointed them out. But it was not the names he wanted me to see — it was the dates on the headstones — and now that I was paying attention to them, they leapt out at me. The dates ranged from the 1700s to the 1920s. Save for some graves with plastic Ethiopian flags on them, I could tell no one brought flowers, and the grass was mowed only once in a while.

'It makes me think the bond of killing together is stronger than the bond of life,' he said, looking at the flags. He added that every now and then a veteran's association paid someone to bring fresh flowers and flags to their long-ago dead.

'Killing together or defending together?' I asked him.

'Is there a difference in the end? Those attacking will also end up in their own graveyards,' he answered.

'Okay. But why are we here?' I asked, even though in the quietness surrounded by so much life, I could sense why.

'This graveyard, we found it here abandoned. The people lying here beneath us, they could be my great-great-grandparents. It makes me think, in a hundred years from now, another you could be standing on mine,' he answered thoughtfully.

'So?' I asked him.

'I am trying to say something that will make sense of all this — that we are here and then we are gone. Knowing a hundred years from now, even my grave will not have anyone to tend to it, does it matter what my parents, Mrs. Hughes or Maaza say?' he asked rhetorically.

'Okay, go on, tell me,' I encouraged him.

'My point is, who remembers the long dead and why? What does it mean to be remembered? Who says that we must all be remembered by our names? If these people were good parents, we might not remember them by name, but they live on, right? Their spirit is still around. What I have learned standing here is that it's okay not to make history. I do not live to be remembered by my name....'

'Then why are you making music? What is the point of it all?' I asked him.

'Man, you are hinting at nihilism. That is not what I am saying, brother. I am saying it's okay to have been alive, to have died and to be forgotten. But I am also telling you that you and me, we will never really be forgotten, because we moved something; we changed someone's life — maybe we gave something, or we took something. The things we touch, even though our fingerprints will be erased by time...our imprint carries on, changes form, maybe, but it's there...,' he explained animatedly.

'So? Are you saying we accomplish just by being born then?' I asked him.

'By being born, we change the future. But I mean a little bit more than that. I am talking about being freed to be nothing except a good human being. Man, I know I have some talent other people do not have. When I discovered this graveyard, it freed my talent and me. I refuse the pressure of making history.

Mrs. Hughes wants me to make history, and perhaps give her a place in that history. But I want to make music — whether I jam in juke joints or at the fucking Carnegie, I just want to make music. Because I know it's okay to end up in untended, unmarked graves.'

He took the bottle of Chivas, took a swig and, unlike Bekele's father, poured a generous libation. 'That is why I came to the ABC, for the music, not for history,' he added, before I could ask him.

'Would you say the same thing if you were not rich?' I asked him, well aware of the irony.

'All the more reason, actually,' he said with a laugh.

I could almost see it: The Diva, The Corporal, The Taliban Man and Miriam — the Tizita — it was about the music, not living the life of a musician, but being a musician. Music is life; life is music. The Tizita is life; life is the Tizita. And you go where life, which is also the Tizita, leads you, even if it's the ABC or the juke joint or a stadium full of people.

'By the way, The Diva said I should tell you she wants to bring you in,' I said, remembering her curious request.

He laughed. 'What were her exact words?'

'"Bring you in" — she would not say into what, or from where,' I answered, not knowing what difference it made.

'Bringing me in from the cold — play on Bob's "Coming from the Cold." But what the fuck does she mean?' he asked.

'Not sure I am the right person—'

'Oh, come on, man!' he protested.

'You want her in your corner. She is a world unto herself — if

I was to think of one person the god of music would be scared of, it's her. There is much to learn from her — like how to reconcile all the yous into one you,' I answered, using words I would not use in my article. In my write-up, I would probably say she is the consummate musician's musician.

'Is that what she is doing for you? Bro, you are in love, smitten. Damn, what did she do to you?' he joked, but I could tell he knew what I meant.

'I can share my graveyard philosophy with her,' he added, as we took several sips (for the road, he said) and went back to the house.

From a distance, it sounded like the party had quieted down, as instrumental music from the house band drifted to us.

'My friends sometimes pass out early — call it taking a nap — before carrying on,' The Taliban Man explained.

21

*'He pitied me for not knowing absolute love,
giving it and receiving it.'*

Fuck! We got back to a sex party! There were a number of empty beer cartons full of condoms and all sorts of lubricants, some edible and some that glow in the dark. The band was now playing an instrumental version of Tina Turner's "What's Love Got to Do with It." The partiers were in all sorts of positions and penetrations, glowing penises and confetti on breasts. It looked like sculptures of squirming bodies strewn all over the backyard. The Taliban Man tucked on a glowing condom and went off to join one of the sculptures.

One of the women I had been introduced to much earlier, and thought pretty in an abstract kind of way, came up to me. It was a quick decision. With all that I had seen and experienced over the last few days, and here with the cool kids, what choice did I really have?

I gathered she had been closing in on her orgasm before wanting to switch partners. Just as well, because I did not last long. We came together, and she was off to another partner, leaving me out of breath, embarrassed as my glowing condom threatened to fall off my limp dick.

Before I could stand up to leave, there was a man's mouth on my dick – it was Binyam. I willed myself to get excited – nothing. I tried to explain it was not him, that I am a one-shot kinda guy, that there is no way I am going to come to an orgy full of beautiful people and leave so soon, but I am done. And I really wanted to, to be part of the energy, to give back, so to speak, I added. Besides, a mouth is a mouth – on a dick, it has no gender, and it still felt good – I was just done.

'Did you prepare?' he asked with casual concern.

'Prepare?'

'For anal?'

'You have to prepare for that?' I asked him, sounding so surprised that he did a double take.

'Damn, what does the Repo-Man know?' he said as he guided my hand to his dick.

'Now, this I don't need to prep...plenty of practice,' I said to him as I jerked him off, watching his pleasure join the chorus all around us.

After he was done, he strode off energetically and still hard to another couple. I threw my used, cold condom into the wastebasket as someone walked out from the kitchen with fresh homemade popcorn. I stood around and watched jealously for a few minutes before calls for Repo-Man to join one scene or another started. With nothing to offer, I made my way to the pool.

After washing my sticky hands, I dipped my feet in, waiting for a floating bottle of whisky to ebb and flow my way. I heard a splash, and a few seconds later, something tugged at my toes. I screamed and fell into the pool, thinking the indignities would never end. The culprit, it turned out, was Maaza.

'I figured you needed a bath,' she teased me.

'Yeah, an orgy is no country for old men,' I replied, thinking there was no point in hiding the obvious.

'Great movie,' she said.

'Not your scene, I take it?' I asked as I climbed back to land.

'No, not really. Been there, done that – all of that – my undergrad. Now, I like my sex the way I like my basketball – one-on-one and with as little dribbling as possible,' she answered.

I knew the line – from the spoof movie *Naked Gun,* and so we spoke about movies for a while.

'We should make out,' she suddenly said, to my surprise.

'Why?'

'Just because we can,' she answered.

So we did, in a very *high schoolish* way, until we started laughing. Ours was not a sexual connection, and the joy was in trying to make it one from the safety of knowing that. The 'orgists' trickled back onto the dance floor, a zipper or a bra needing adjusting every now and then. And we carried on.

How would I explain what had just happened to my readers? And how far would I be willing to go in the telling? Yes, when you looked at it, it was sex across genders, straight and gay. I mean, I had just jerked off a dude for the first time in my life, and watching the growing pleasure on his face was beautiful, as it had been with the woman, as it was watching all the writhing sculptures in the garden. We were humans giving each other another form of pleasure. To me, that moment — it felt like it really was just as life should be. It was life. The beauty of it, of writing for a tabloid, was that it was, for the reader, going to be truth and fiction, and therefore I would tell everything.

* * *

I was woken up by a text from Alison in the morning. I had maxed out *The National Inquisitor*'s credit card. I was not sure where all the money (1,000 dollars, she said) had gone, but I had been eating and drinking well these past few days, and generous with buying. I called her to ask for more — no way! My story had done well, but not well enough to justify 'bottomless expenditure.' She asked me how much material I had gathered, and I told her enough for two profiles. She wanted me to go back to Nairobi and have in-depth interviews with The Corporal when he came for the final competition. But I knew that would not work; when we travel, we become other people. It was the listening and observing in place that I wanted.

I did not have enough in my savings to keep me going. So I did the one thing I had never done since I returned from Boston: I called my mother to ask for more money. She did not give me a lecture about fiscal responsibility, as she would have done in the past. Or hand the phone over to my father for the same lecture. She did not even ask me where I was, but I explained anyway. As it turned out, she had read my write-up and found it 'of interest.' My mother reading *The National Inquisitor*? I guess I was pulling them into the gutter one by one. She asked me how much, and in less than 30 minutes, she had wired 2,000 dollars into my bank account. There was a small price to pay, though: I was to spend a whole weekend with them out in Nakuru when I returned. I was looking forward to seeing both of them. Our relationship had always been reflexive, they trying to reel me in and I avoiding them, but it felt like it was the right time to spend time with them. Even get answers to a few questions I had never dared ask.

I got off the phone and walked and looked around, expecting a war zone. But The Taliban Man's place was immaculately clean. His maids had cleaned up after we passed out. All the debris was gone, and only bodies in various stages of undress remained. What was left on display was a group of young people who could literally do anything. I had never seen so much talent and promise in one room. Feeling less optimistic than I had yesterday, I could not help but wonder, through the fog of my unfolding brain, how much of this talent was going to eventually go to waste — overdoses, alcoholism, drug addictions, the occasional suicide and, even worse, being co-opted into corrupt governance. The level of intensity I had witnessed was not sustainable. As in the apartheid generation of the Can Thembas and Arthur Nortjes, there were bound to be a few casualties.

I walked into the dining room and found The Taliban Man playing his electric guitar, headphones hooked into the amp. It reminded me of the naked Diva on her piano, only he was wearing a bathrobe and sandals. I stood there watching him for a while, listening to the almost silent sound of an intricate web of various forms of music — he was slipping in and out of jazz, into afro-beat, sometimes into merengue, which he would slow down to salsa. It was like watching an athlete doing a workout. It occurred to me he was trying to tap into something deeper than music or, rather, into a river of sound from which all music draws its form, dip into it and rise up with a sound that was his own — not because it was original and new, but because it had found some unsaid things, some unsounded things that he could add to the language of music. And to get there, he had to speak all the languages of music he knew.

Maaza woke up from wherever she had passed out and joined me. Still a bit groggy, she leaned onto my shoulder, I embraced her and we watched her brother trying to find footing in the otherwise fast-moving river of muted sounds. I started to hear it, and so did Maaza, because she leaned deeper into me: his own sound that he was yet to own. He was humming along now — anticipating a note, or sometimes following something he had just played. It was there — an infant sound learning from the languages of Fela Kuti, Beethoven, Ali Farka, Mahmood Ahmed, Bezawork, Nina Simone. It was there. The foetus (Maaza's words, not mine) was alive and kicking.

Abruptly, he cursed aloud and stopped playing. He held up his fingers to his eyes. They were bleeding. He attempted to play again, but the pain was too much, and he stopped and just cradled the guitar. I started to walk in to ask him about that sound, but Maaza stopped me.

'He is still playing, in his head,' she explained as she walked me outside for my ride back to my hotel room. I had to start working on The Corporal's write-up anyway.

Mustafa and The Diva happened to be rolling in to see The Taliban Man as I was getting back into the red limo. Mustafa asked me if I wanted to wait around, and they would drop me off. I said no and wished them all the best.

'So, what do you think of The Taliban Man?' The Diva asked me.

'You need him on your label, and he needs you,' I replied.

'Another believer —that makes two of us,' she said with a laugh.

'See you both in Nairobi,' I said curtly and hopped into the red limo, feeling strangely depressed.

I could feel tears of wanting — of just wanting, of hunger — welling up. As the driver started the car and I took out my notes and laptop, I realised I did not want to do this alone, that I could not do this alone. I asked the limo driver to wait. He did not ask why. I found Maaza and asked her whether she would like to come with me to see The Corporal, and she said no. Close to tears, I begged her to come with me. I needed a translator, someone who would help me navigate, but deep down, it was because I did not want to be alone; my wounds untended would bleed me to death.

'Just know I am not interested in you,' she said to agree.

'You have no reason to worry. I am, as you know, already spent. It takes me one week to recover,' I said to cheer both of us up, feeling relieved and grateful.

What was it that Mohamed had told me the night of the bonfire to the heavens? He pitied me for not having children. He pitied me for not knowing absolute love, giving it and receiving it. Those words came back at me more forcefully than he had said them. But it was what he had said that was hurting: that we miss those things that we don't know. It was not because I wanted children per se, or a house in the suburbs with a saloon and another one in my village with a pick-up truck parked outside. It was the being haunted by all the nameless things I could feel missing.

22

The Corporal

'Your Corporal is a war criminal who should be tried at Nuremberg.'

'What do you mean that piece of shit is a musician? He is just a mean son of a bitch who loves killing. Music? Music? No!' Jember Belendia was saying angrily. JB, as he insisted we call him, was tall, balding and portly, but with a thin face and freckled brown skin. 'But I guess the most fertile place to plant a seed is in shit,' he added with mock contemplation. JB had served in the army with The Corporal.

Maaza and I were having lunch at a small bar kiosk in Dejen, a small, poor town on the outskirts of Addis where we were to meet The Corporal.

'The trick to good food is eating at this kind of place. Grandma's cooking — the real thing, not trying to cater to the city middle class,' she was saying as she tore some injera and scooped some chicken doro wot from her side of the round serving platter — her territory, I joked.

That was when, through the door, I noticed a man circling her BMW whistling and gently running his fingers along its contours. I pointed him out him to Maaza; she smiled and acquired more territory on the plate. The Maaza who was expensively dressed the night before was now wearing a long, simple blue dress, her hair down, no makeup and looking fresh in spite of the hard night. I was in my journalist uniform, a black shirt, brown corduroys and my safari boots. The man, when he walked in, would turn out to be JB. One of those moments, pure coincidence, which we love as journalists — it means you are in the story, or the story is finding you.

'Why do you write for a tabloid? You can tell me; I won't judge,' Maaza asked, moving away from culinary talk.

I wanted to tell her about how I had received a letter from Mr. Mbugua, my very own Mrs. Hughes, in which he could not hide his disdain at my working for a tabloid. This was all the more hurtful because I had just done a big story on how wealthy old politicians in their quest for perpetual youth were misusing Viagra so much that parliament had to shut down when MP after MP stood to address the venerable body with a hard on. In his letter addressed to the editor, Mr. Mbugua had written that he had always hoped I would become a serious fiction writer, a family doctor or (boldly hinted) an English primary school teacher like himself.

I had considered becoming a writer in the past, even applying to Iowa's Writing Workshop, where my literary hero, Meja Mwangi, had sharpened his pen, but they did not even bother writing me a rejection letter. Soon after that, I applied to journalism schools, and Boston University took me in. I did not write Mr. Mbugua back, but if I were to do it now, it would be to tell him that we are born many things and then we become one.

But I did not tell her all that — that his letter still disturbed me, the idea that he would feel he had wasted his knowledge on me.

'For the same reason you do poor law,' I said instead.

'Poor law!' she scoffed, but she let me continue.

'Anger, I think. Because of my parents, I had access to the private lives of the politicians. On TV they appear put together, invincible. But I had their dirt — little things, but really nasty stuff. No paper wanted to touch that. I wanted to expose them. But along the way, I have been coming across people doing interesting things — ordinary people — like this crazy guy who earns his drinks reading the daily newspaper like a TV news broadcaster in a bar....'

'Can you do it?' she asked. As I mimed, to her amusement, a broadcast about a long dormant volcano suddenly erupting, the man from outside came in and asked if that was our car outside. After Maaza answered, he asked if we were married, and she said no, we were just friends.

'You can't fool me; you are obviously a couple,' he said with knowing winks. 'What brings you to my town?'

Then he asked what we do, and she said that we were journalists and were writing a story about The Corporal and his music. Perhaps he knew him? And that is when JB shouted, 'Your Corporal is a war criminal who should be tried at Nuremberg.'

'The Hague,' I corrected him, but he continued on.

They had served together in the Ogaden war. The Somalis,

cut up by the Italians and the British and parcelled out to Kenya and Ethiopia, were waging a unification war. But neither Kenya nor Ethiopia wanted to give up their colonial borders for ones that made sense. Several massacres, like the Wagalla massacres committed by the Kenyan army against Kenyan Somalis, left hundreds dead, and still nothing resolved. Somalia eventually descended into anarchy and piracy — of course, that resolved nothing. Perhaps with national integrity, the country would have survived itself, but already parcelled out and under siege, collapse was inevitable.

Now, of course, JB did not put it quite this way. He saw the Somalis as ungrateful for all the Ethiopians had done for them. And, rather conveniently, he invoked pan-Africanism to say that Africa needed to unite and not form borders along ethnicity. But still, what The Corporal did went beyond the call of duty. So much so that even his fellow soldiers and commanding officers feared him. We were intrigued. He ordered a round of *tej*, honey beer, for us all as he settled in.

'The Corporal — there is no courage in that man. We once captured this Somali kid, no more than 16 years old, but he could handle an AK. We captured him, and we were loading him into our army truck. Suddenly, a grenade in the truck. You know what your Corporal does? He picks up the kid and throws him on the grenade. We survive, but the kid has a crater for a stomach. He is still alive, and I take out my pistol to finish him off. But The Corporal, he tells me not to waste a bullet. And he stands there and watches him die. He has a smile on his face, like he is watching the son he does not have get married. I am angry, and I curse him. Next thing I know, he is holding a gun to my head. He forces me to thank him. Forces all of us to thank him. Later, he gets a commendation for his quick thinking.'

He drank his tej fast, as if to chase down the nasty taste of the memory. I joined him, as did Maaza. We all needed to chase down history with a drink.

'We all died that day — every one of us. We are soldiers — we killed many more after that. But him, he liked to kill in order, starting from the bottom up,' he said.

'What do you mean?' I asked him as I ordered us another round.

'He finds a family. He starts by killing the least, the smallest — a cat, a dog, a goat, a cow, small children, until only the mother or father is left. He called it the bottom-up method,' he explained, tears that seemed independent of his matter-of-fact narration rolled down his face.

I must have been missing something in translation — it did not sound like The Corporal at the ABC, the Tizita musician. I was not sure if I believed JB — wars happen, and soldiers torture, kill and commit atrocities. But this was Nazi shit, something that went beyond sadism to become evil personified by The Corporal. Was it that I did not want to believe it?

But why would JB lie? Our meeting had been purely accidental, so it was not like he had time to prepare such an extreme story, and why that story, as opposed to another, more believable one? If true, it would certainly make for a better story. I was going to keep listening.

'I am sorry for asking this — he did save your lives after all, no?' I pressed him as I reached to put my hand on his shoulder, which he brushed off.

'It was the kind of saving that kills, you understand? It's like a child dying to save the parent. The parent dies too. I mean, look at me,' he said, as he forcefully poked himself in the chest.

'If I had to do it all over again, I would jump on that grenade. A musician? The Corporal? I can only laugh. He cannot sing his sins away,' JB added, more to himself.

He ordered another glass for himself. As soon as it arrived, The Corporal walked in, and I saw fear slowly spreading all over JB's face. Torn between running and finishing his drink, he chose the latter and, with his ever-widening eyes on The Corporal, he gulped down his drink. The Corporal walked over to the server-bartender to say hello, and they talked for a minute or so. JB finished his drink and tried to bravely walk out. But The Corporal opened his arms wide, started to smile and then broke into laughter, the sort of laughter that comes with not having seen someone for a very long time, a friend from another life. The Corporal hugged JB, slapped his back a few times. JB returned the greetings, with a bit of embarrassment, but just as enthusiastically — and then, as soon as he looked back to Maaza and me, the fear returned.

'Did JB tell you our war stories?' the beaming Corporal asked, turning to us.

'Yes, he told us how you saved their lives,' Maaza answered, looking at me, and I at The Corporal.

'Is that so? JB is being too modest — he would have done the same in my place,' he answered, without missing a beat. 'JB, my friend, my brother, you must have a beer on me.'

Maaza translated as JB turned it down with effusive excuses. The Corporal insisted, and he relented.

'Thank you, Corporal. I will drink it first thing in the morning.'

He had quickly come up with a solution, and I admired him for that. The Corporal laughed and told the server-bartender to keep a bottle of beer in reserve for JB. I did not realise it then, but sly or fearful, JB had left us with the bill for the rounds he bought for us.

The Corporal, dressed in a cheap brown suit, had all along been standing, and he politely asked if he could sit down with us. As I introduced Maaza to him, she had a contemplative look on her face, as if trying to figure out which of the emerging, competing stories was true. The Corporal, now appearing slim to the point of fragility, was hard to reconcile with the murdering soldier painted by JB. I asked him if he would like anything, and he ordered tej. He was ready to get started.

23

'Sound — I think The Corporal was trying to tell me — expresses that archive, a 200,000-year-old archive of extreme human emotions.'

My journalistic instincts told me that The Corporal was the sort of man for whom you had to find the right word, the right question and the right phrasing to open him up. No bullshit, no warming up to a conversation.

'Corporal, I want to start by giving you one word only: Tizita,' I said to him.

'If I did not play music, I would be like JB. Unable to do anything for myself except drink. War — we go to war; war is death.... We come back to life, and we find we are already dead. We cannot respect life if we know that someone can take it easily. Music? The Tizita brought me to life,' was his immediate response.

I suspected he brought up the war first because he knew JB would have spoken to us about it. I was glad he did because it created an opening to ask the harder questions later.

'But what is it about music that does that?' Maaza asked him, translating her question for me.

'The only true thing in this life is sound; the one thing that can take you back is sound,' he answered.

'Back to and from where?' she asked, and he looked at me as if to ask who was doing the interview. I nodded to agree with her question.

'Back to the beginning. If you think about it, in the womb there is no light, only sound, the mother's beating heart, for example. The child patterns his heartbeat after the mother's. Life is sound; it does not matter if you are as deaf as a stone, you feel sound, the beat — and you build your life around this sound, this beat. You walk, run and shit on it; you live and kill to it; you make love and kill to it — always to sound. Sound is more than rhythm; sound is everything. The soul.'

'The soul — isn't that a bit vague?' I asked.

'Because it is unknown. We want to call it unknown because that is easy. Think about the first death — the Tizita, to me, for me, is that sound of the first death, the recognition and the surprise and the realisation; that first consciousness that realised it was going to be no more — and it wanted to leave a message in a bottle that becomes me and you. With the Tizita, I can feel it; I know it, but I cannot speak it. So I sing the Tizita, because it will echo in your soul, sound waves from yesterday meeting yours and, perhaps, we shall understand something that we do not have words for yet. All I can say is, you can walk for a very long time and get to where you are going, but all along, little bits of yourself are left along the way, and you get to where you are going, and there is no going back without stepping on yourself, and there is no going forward without eventually tearing your entrails out of your body. The Tizita is that impossibility — I am dead and buried, and I am alive and well at the same time. When I sing it, I know what that is, even though when I stop, I cannot explain it — an understanding with no words, only sound.' He stopped and looked at Maaza and me, waiting for his words to sink in or for the follow up question.

Echoes — he sounded a little bit like The Diva and her idea of the Tizita carrying traces of that first light. And yet, it was not a return to the beginning — it was to feel echoes of a series of first *violences* and beauties — the big bang, the first birth, the first death, the first love and down through the years. If the Tizita was like the wind, it would be whipping across these sediments of violent and beautiful firsts, echoing them into the present. Just last week, before coming to Ethiopia, I knew of the Tizita as an archive of the past, but now I was beginning to understand it in a more fundamental way.

Let me put it this way: historians record history — and even though there are competing versions, it is there on paper. In science, each new discovery and invention is directly tied to the previous one, an archive that is also new. But human emotion, feeling — where is the archive? Philosophy and psychology explain. But where is the archive that we can visit to learn about what the first human being felt on first experiencing love or the tragedy of losing a loved one? That first parent to bury their child? We fall in love, and it feels like it's for the first time; we assume the emotion of love does not contain the archive of past loves, from generation to generation, all the way back to that living thing that first gruffly grunted, 'I see, I love.' Sound — I think The Corporal was trying to tell me —

expresses that archive, a 200,000-year-old archive of extreme human emotions.

'Anything else?' The Corporal asked, looking at his watch. I needed to win him over if I was going to get to talk about the JB, the war and music beyond what he had rehearsed. I had to give him something.   I weighed my losses – which one would draw out The Corporal? My dead uncle cut to pieces by thugs?   My own mother's indiscretions with the dictator? Stories of madness from the belly of Babylon? What story? Then it hit me, a loss that was mine – one I could not account for.

'You know, Corporal, when I lived in Boston, something happened. I dated this girl; I loved her, but we were both damaged. We broke up, you know...she left me. Months later, we met and she said she was pregnant, with a boy. She had an abortion....'

He looked interested. 'It is life – but what did you do?' he asked.

'We fucked and cried. I realised how much I loved her then. Then, in the morning, she left, and I never heard from her again. Often I wonder about that – this other life–'

'Maybe she had no choice. Or it was what she wanted, and it had nothing to do with you,' Maaza interrupted.

'Maybe, I know – I know most probably it was the right thing to do, for her anyway, but still, I wonder about that other life I could have lived – wife, son, writing for *The New York Times*.... Sometimes, I want it so bad that this life I am living seems like the lie. When I think of that other life, I feel like it is out there, another me living it, but I have no words for it. And I think I hear its echoes when I am listening to the Tizita,' I said, thinking that adding that bit about echoes of that life was a nice touch. It is not that I was jaded; I knew, sensed so much, and I wanted more of the story. My hunger had become manipulative — or I was finally doing my job.

'Yes, that is exactly it, my friend — to know something and not have words for it — only sound can carry that; you can hear that other life and feel it through music!' he exclaimed, putting his hand on my shoulder.

'But there is more to the Tizita. It is not just about loss; it's more than that. The Tizita is about life, living in this hard world, of drawing water out of a rock, or turning a mirage into water. The Tizita is about life, all of it,' he tried to explain. I had no response to that.

'But, my friend, why don't you?' The Corporal then asked.

'Do what?'

'Live that other life — you know what I mean?'

'I wouldn't be here,' I answered.

'But you would be there,' he said, and we all started laughing. 'I better get you another beer,' he added.

'Do you think he is a war criminal?' I asked Maaza as he went to the counter.

'Hard to tell — but then, what do war criminals look like?' she asked simply. 'There is no innocence when it comes to us.'

I should have, but I did not ask what she meant.

The Corporal returned with three beers, one for Maaza and

one for me, toasted and slammed his glass on the table, rubbed his hands on his trousers and blew on them as if to cool them down.

'For a musician, the beat' — he drummed the table, a syncopated staccato, like he was playing the conga drums — 'the beat consumes him, and it becomes all he hears, total immersion, a total darkness before he continues; the beat is life itself.'

'Tizita, in the end, is about life, yet you were a soldier. The war, how did the war influence your music?' I asked him, feeling it was the right time to get to his war experiences.

'Trench warfare in the twenty-first century. I never quite understood it, but we fought, killed and stayed alive. But on this one day, we rushed an enemy camp. I took aim and shot an Eritrean soldier. I felt a sharp burning pain on my right thigh; I had just been shot. I could have continued fighting, but the sight of my blood and the exhaustion — I was done.

'I sat down and tended to my wound, watching the rush of soldiers killing each other. When the fighting quieted down, I rolled over the body of my kill. I knew the face; though bloodied, he looked familiar. It was probably a soldier I had fought alongside to get rid of our common enemy, Mengistu, just a few years before. I deserted that evening,' he narrated without much emotion, like he was telling a story he had told hundreds of times before.

I did not say it, but I knew the reason he had not answered the question was because that was the myth he wanted me to tell the world. I started to ask him about the alleged atrocities, but he saw it coming.

'Let's save war talk for later,' he said and stood up to leave. 'Bottoms up,' he said in English and laughed, finished his tej and left to go set up at a local juke joint.

Maaza and I looked at each other, trying to gauge each other's thoughts.

She said it aloud first. 'It's a good story. It's a fucking amazing story.'

The server-bartender whom we had not paid any mind came to us. We really should not believe every word from JB, he said. I asked him if he could tell us anything about The Corporal to contradict JB's account.

'That is all I am willing to say,' he said, more cautiously than fearfully.

Maaza asked him if he had been in the army as well. Instead, he told us to talk to The Corporal's CO. You know, his commanding officer. He had no idea where to find him, though, and I was not so sure it was worth the trouble trying to find him. I wrote for a tabloid after all, and I could take liberties with a story that your *Nation* reporter could not.

'The Corporal is a great musician. He is also a great man,' he said as we settled our bill.

We stepped outside. The sun was setting, dark clouds around its girth, bright-red-yet-dark rays coming through as if from behind a massive, greyish screen. Maaza and I held hands, the joints from her piano fingers pressing against mine. If we were kids, we would have been skipping, walking and singing, only in our story, the Tizita tears us apart. We liked it here.

24

'The Tizita is selfish — it just wants to be sung.'

The Corporal's juke joint — unlike The Diva's, which was more like a neighbourhood joint — was a place for African transplants in Addis. Indeed, it was called the Amakwerekwere Joint, referring to what our xenophobic South African sisters and brothers call African immigrants because their languages are undecipherable to the sensitive South African ear: *Amakwerekwere*. Unsurprisingly, there is a mixture of five distinct smells in almost equal parts — mint tea, charcoal burner, weed, stale/fermented alcohol and roasting goat meat.

Maaza and I settled in with drinks as The Corporal held court centre stage. He was playing his masenko with a three-piece band composed of a krar player, a drummer and a bassist. His band mates were much older than he was. The bassist, for example, appeared to be well into his eighties. Where the relatively younger krar player did some furious footwork so that a fusillade of sound captured pain, anger and loss, the older bassist took his time, bending his strings into a heavy multisyllabic rising and falling pentameter — what I imagine peacefulness would sound like, if it had a rhythm.

The Corporal called up a young woman who had been sitting by herself surrounded by coats and walking sticks piled on plastic chairs. She was the bassist's daughter, it turned out, and even though they did not say it, I could tell she was an apprentice. It is like a young football player being called in to play because the game had already been won, or irretrievably lost — might as well give them some practice. She took the bass from her father, who kissed her on her cheek as he left the stage. The drummer eased the band into a slow song — and she slipped on the bass.

Then something went wrong, and everything was out of sync — the bass, she had not found the grooves to play her bass along. The krar tried to make a headway into the sound of the band, but it ended up sounding like amplified termites drilling into dry wood — fast, busy, with a low buzz of activity as they hollow out everything. The drummer, unsure of what was happening, kept working. And that was when The Corporal came in with his masenko — he kept the beat with his one-stringed devil until the bassist caught up. He slowed down when she ran ahead and sped up when she lagged behind until she finally found her walking pace within the band. And then, her youth serving her, she started driving the bass through the spaces left wide open by the older, experienced players, and she emerged from the background to take the lead.

She led with the bass until the band came to rest on a song I recognised: "I Would Rather Go Blind." She was singing it in Amharic, her voice deep, reminding one of a young Mavis

Staples, a voice made for the blues. They had found their grooves, and they took us on a long, 20-minute song journey. At some point, a young man joined them for a duet — him singing in isiXhosa, the different clicks adding to the beat of the song. This brought out the soft Amharic clicks, made them more pronounced. In The Corporal's juke joint, we were in a Tower of Babel — an underclass one where there were no high-end languages and instruments, just people who loved music, who could play it well, for whom music meant life, getting together and jamming — music the soundtrack in the Tower of Babel.

They played on as Maaza and I joined the old bassist at the bar — he smelt of tobacco and worked as a manager at a coffee plantation.

'I hear you are writing a story about The Corporal,' he said, pleasantly enough, which made what he said next all the more surprising.

'Your Corporal is not the real Corporal. Think Sonny Boy Williamson as a ringer for the real Sonny Boy Williamson? Sonny Boy Williamson II, born Alex Miller, vs the real Sonny Boy Williamson, the original one, a mean harmonica player. Alex Miller, tall, handsome, and also gifted with the harmonica. He named himself Sonny Boy Williamson II, and easily overshadowed the original. Think Corporal I and Corporal II. This Corporal, he is good. But the real Corporal, the one who died in the war alongside all his men, he was the best,' the old man told Maaza and me.

The way I understood it, it was not like Elvis stealing Big Mama Thornton's song; it was a case of Elvis actually becoming

Big Mama Thornton, and so much so that he erased her. Sonny
Boy Williamson II effectively erased Sonny Boy Williamson I.

'How can that be?' Maaza asked him.

'I have heard from people I know very well, soldiers in the
war, there was a corporal — the best masenko player to ever
live — he died in the war alongside his whole unit. That one' —
and he waved at The Corporal — 'is an imposter.'

'Are you sure?' I asked him.

'No, but how can anyone be sure?' he returned.

'DNA, dental records, people who knew the real Corporal,'
Maaza answered.

'What does it matter? He is very good. And the original one
is dead, so he is him now. And in his hands, the masenko is
divine. The masenko came first and then the Tizita. There
would be no Tizita without the masenko. The masenko
discovered the Tizita. And then the Tizita discovered The
Corporal.' He spoke with an old man's patience.

'Then why tell us if it does not matter?' I asked him.

'The truth in the mouth of a saint or in the mouth of a liar is
always the truth. I told you so you know something important,
so you know that music doesn't care.... The Tizita is selfish —
it just wants to be sung,' he explained with his palms on our
hands like he was leading us into prayer.

Maaza looked at me and laughed. There was a part of me
that did not care, as well. The Corporal lent himself very well
to *The National Inquisitor*. In my write-up, I could focus on
any one of his myths. The bassist had this smile, like he had
accomplished his mission. And later, Maaza would tell me she

had laughed because she caught him winking at The Corporal.

It is possible he was creating these stories to keep us from getting to the truth of who he is. When a military helicopter comes under fire from a heat-seeking missile, the pilot will deploy flares — a countermeasure that misdirects the missile. The multiple stories could very well be The Corporal's countermeasure.

But all the same, with that many conflicting stories, there had to be something enigmatic about him. I did not need the truth; what I needed were the stories.

The Corporal and the bassist's daughter played on for a while. The band retired; it was bedtime for the old musicians, The Corporal joked.

The Corporal almost fell down as he stood up to get another beer (to go, he said). It was time to leave. He was way too drunk to get home by himself — as we were too drunk to drive, but Maaza drove anyway — and through potholes that aggravated my stomach every time we hit one. We made it to his house, a one-bedroom apartment with a short winding path that went through a well-kept garden, in contrast to the small houses and apartments around his. There was no electricity, and we stumbled to his doorstep, where we found all sorts of dead and dying rodents. He stepped over them and invited us in.

'My cat — when I have been away, it likes to leave me gifts. Cats are wild animals, like us,' he said and lit a kerosene lamp. He found a bottle of an unlabelled something that smelled like whisky and three tin cups.

I asked him what the 20-minute-long song was all about, explaining it was reminiscent of Kidane's hour-plus-long song at The Diva's juke joint.

'The Tizita never rests, man,' he answered. 'The Tizita is always hungry. I try to feed it, but sometimes it just spits whatever I am trying to feed it back at me. But I want to keep trying — and why not? I think the people who listen to me want me to keep trying — it's the trying they want, not the success. Look, man, there are all sorts of music — you know who created a three-minute song? The recording company. Fela Kuti — his best music — take "Sorrow Tears and Blood"— which one do you listen to? The 30-minute or three-minute version? The Tizita, you want it from many angles, and for that you have to play it for a long time,' he explained, appearing relaxed for the first time.

'What do you mean? Even if you record a 50-minute song, it is still on record, no? It will always be the same?' I followed up.

'No, it's not. A 50-minute Fela is a journey. The ending changes the beginning; the middle will change the ending; the beginning will be something else by the time you get to the end. Its possibilities are infinite. A long song is a lifetime, my brother...a lifetime,' he said and started drifting off.

'Or a lifeline,' Maaza added after a beat of silence.

'Can we talk about the war?' I asked. He laughed — not self-consciously or to mask shame. He was amused.

'You expect to find humanity in war? You go to war to become a better person? In war, you give yourself to it, or you get taken. But I do not want to talk about the war; I want to talk about music,' he answered.

'Do you know of a young man called Bekele, probably in the army at the same time you were?' I pushed on.

'No, I don't recall,' he evaded. 'I know of many Bekeles though. The name is not very unique.'

'He was a soldier. He came back; after a little while, he shot himself in the head,' I clarified.

For the first time, I saw The Corporal lose his cool. He coughed into his drink and put it down slowly.

'Yes, I knew him. We were in the same company; we fought together. He was a brave young man,' he answered.

'Do you know why he killed himself?'

'War — no one really comes back. If it were not for my music, where would I be? Only God knows.'

I looked at him to see if there were any signs betraying remorse, or fear of being found out, anything, but he appeared more morose than anything.

'You fight long enough, and only the war matters. You find meaning in the worst of things. To survive, your humanity has to be a notch lower than anyone else's. You understand?'

I decided to ask him about the other Corporal, the supposedly real one. I could see the violence in him rising up. Then he regained control. He looked at Maaza and me as if contemplating something.

'Here, follow me — I want to show you something,' he said, and we followed him to the sitting room.

He rolled up a carpet and opened a trapdoor.

'In the mountains, during the war, we dug tunnels. It's okay, come on in,' he encouraged on, seeing the look of surprise and concern on our faces.

We followed him down what I can only call a path to a poorly dug cave. There were two chests covered with dusty plastic paper. He opened them. They were full of weapons, naturally.

'He is sane and crazy at the same time,' Maaza whispered to me.

'The war never ends,' he said, even before we could ask.

'There is always a war, but does yours ever end?' I asked him as I found a dusty post to lean against.

He looked at both of us — and here you really have to see it to get it. The moment we had been driving to all day and night — Maaza pulling back the plastic and running her fingers over the weapons like the war she had been fighting in the Addis courtrooms had become real, or reduced to simple violence. You have to see me, curious and interested, but scared, not for my life (physical danger was not it) — it was fear of seeing something that could undo everything, fear I could not contain it.

And you have to picture the fucking dug-out cave and The Corporal, torn between having revealed too much and wanting to reveal more and hating what to him must have seemed like our bourgeoisie, protected lives, and him wondering why it had to be us.

You have to see the cave itself — floor slightly muddy, nothing is finished, a one-man effort, a space that will never look better. You have to see how we keep moving around the small cave for position — there could be no comfort; Maaza putting her hair into a ponytail, me seeing her and running my hands across my hair to get rid of the soil, and The Corporal just fucking intense, himself a weapon, contained like a grenade.

'You see this?' he asked, pointing at an old-looking AK-47.

'This is the gun I killed the real Corporal with — he was a real son of a bitch, someone had to put him down. He was the best masenko player I have ever known, but the war — it drove him crazy; he killed everything he came across. So I put him down, and I picked up his instrument,' he explained.

It was hard to know what the truth was. It was within the realm of possibility that there had been a real corporal, though that would make JB and the old bassists liars. It was more likely The Corporal viewed his soldier self as another human being, a version of himself he had killed when the war ended. A PTSD-induced complete disassociation?

But then again, what did I really care whether the story he wanted to be true was true? I was not in Ethiopia to cover human rights violations; I was there to talk and write about music. My mandate was a good story. And for Maaza? She could take it wherever she wanted it to go — perhaps there were some generals to sue, families who deserved to know the truth.

'Did you throw an enemy soldier, a young boy, on a grenade to save your men?' Maaza asked him, and I wanted to elbow her into silence after she translated.

The Corporal leaned against the dusty cave wall. 'The other Corporal, he did that — he threw the boy onto a grenade. But he did save our lives.'

'And his bottom-up method?' she followed up.

He looked puzzled, and so Maaza explained, asking, 'Why would JB say it was you? Even you agreed that you saved his life.'

'Did he seem completely sane to you? And how much beer did you buy him?' he asked with a laugh.

'Why are we down here?' I asked, suddenly hit with how tired I was.

'I told you already,' an equally tired Corporal answered. 'All wars have no end.' The Corporal did not have to tell us it was time to leave, and we started for the door. He found a flashlight to walk us back to Maaza's car. And so it was with The Corporal painting a bull's eye on our backs that we left.

* * *

Maaza dropped me off at my hotel. We agreed to have breakfast together and do a recap of our time with The Corporal. I took into my hotel room several competing stories about the origins of the Tizita. All put together, it amounted to the Tizita being a song unique to Ethiopia, sung by wandering griots before the coming of Christianity, but the psalms legitimise it, give it official sanction, if you will. Probably it was the masenko that was the Tizita's instrument of choice, easy to carry and to make. And the masenko then became the instrument to carry the psalms. But it was the krar that was closer to speech, to talking. Slow down the krar, and you can hear a beautiful argumentative conversation; play it fast and it becomes a song.

Regardless of the instrument, there were the singers who

took the Tizita and the masenko back to the world of the secular and caught flack for it. That was as close to the origin as I was going to ever get unless I decided to give up journalism for musical anthropology. And even then, the question would remain — why should we assume something has a single point of origin? If a single origin were possible, wouldn't that be an argument for multiple origins? That if one thing was possible then other things were also possible?

'The Corporal, he is truly a legend,' I had said to Maaza. I believed it.

And I just had to pick one or two of the legends and tell them well. I liked the title "The Tale of the Two Corporals."

I drifted off to sleep.

25

'No bad human being can play a Tizita that well.'

In the morning over breakfast, Maaza insisted that we find The Corporal's CO. I asked why it mattered to her; it was my story after all, and she gave me a look that silenced me.

She made a few calls, negotiated, promised, got into favour-debt and finally we had his name and deployment location — the African Union headquarters, a desk job for his service.

The AU headquarters, magnificent from the outside, did not disappoint on the inside, and we found the CO at the reception desk. It was as you would expect: corporate, clean and efficient. I had not known what to expect, but the CO also looked the part, dressed in an old, faded, grey-striped suit; polished, aged leather shoes; his grey hair smoothed backwards and overly white teeth that suggest they might be false. But his only visible eccentricity — a long, greying, braided beard — told me that, like The Taliban Man's Mrs. Hughes, they kept him around for some reason. It signalled some sort of power — could be persuasion, could be the power of mockery, giving African heads of state walking by something to have a quick laugh about.

He was ready for us, he said, and we stepped outside and sat on a stone bench, a water fountain in front of us. With soldierly precision, he unpacked a steak sandwich and opened his can of coke. Thanks to Miriam's connections, he had an idea why we were there, and after an exchange of more pleasantries, I wanted to ask him about The Corporal, telling him what JB had told us.

He liked taking his time, like someone thinking as they talked. 'The first thing you need to know is that The Corporal is...was...a soldier's soldier. He served under me, but it was my privilege and honour to have him under my command,' he said with pride.

'He was a soldier's soldier,' he attempted to explain, but I looked at him puzzled. 'Okay, let me give you an example, something I saw with my own eyes,' he said, his voice muffled as he bit into his sandwich. 'You want to know? I will tell you. We were just a few of us, ten or so. The enemy, about 40 of them, were sleeping. We attacked — element of surprise — we killed a few, wounded a few and captured those that tried to escape. We needed to know what they knew — and we didn't have time. We threatened them; we did bad things to them, broke legs and hands, but they would not talk. The Corporal looked around their camp, and came back with a krar. He asked who played it, and one of the soldiers raised a hand up. The Corporal went to him, raised his pistol to his head. He then gave his pistol to the enemy soldier, who refused to take it.

'The Corporal sat down and started playing. This, in the dead of the night — every sound was like someone was beating a loud drum next to your ear — sound carries. We were used to the sounds of gunfire and screams of torture. He started playing a Tizita. It was like watching a child being born, but not in a hospital. It was like a child being born during a war. He played, and he reminded us about life, about our wives and children at home...,' he narrated, pride, memory and belief all rolled up in the way he sat, back straight, on the bench.

'Yeah, but that story — I have heard it many times, about many wars,' Maaza said to him.

'As have I,' I added.

'Perhaps so. I am only telling what I saw with my own eyes, my own ears. And aren't all the wars the same? Anyway...the prisoners, they started crying — and they told him everything. How I know it's true is because I would have done the same if the situation were reversed — I would have told him everything. No bad human being can play a Tizita that well.' He kept quiet, as if listening to the Tizita all over again.

'Did The Corporal shoot and kill unarmed civilians and torture prisoners of war? Yes or no?' I pierced through his silence.

'Who didn't? You think missiles and atomic bombs were made to kill ants? Nagasaki, Hiroshima? A soldier is an instrument of war,' he answered with so much derision that I knew we had lost any credibility we might have had.

'Yes, but did he kill civilians?' I asked again, not sure why it mattered. Perhaps outside moral judgement, I just wanted one true thing, as true as it could be without factual corroboration, about The Corporal.

'He saved lives,' he answered.

His lunch break was over. He shook our hands and wished us all the best.

* * *

Why had I been so resistant to the simplest of ideas — that The Corporal could be many things at the same time? Was I not many things, some of them of my own creation? Or The Diva? Or pretty much everyone I knew, except for Maaza, who had rejected multiplicity for singularity?

Was the bassist right? That a song — the Tizita — is selfish; it just wants to be sung? Then why does it give us so much?

'What do you make of it? Would you take The Corporal as a client?' I asked Maaza.

'Fuck. I think I am too old to learn that a fact does not add up to a whole truth, and truth is not moral but ethical...that sin, crime — could have infinite triggers that might actually be good. For a lawyer. I feel fucked and strangely high,' she answered and laughed.

'I hope Miriam's cousin is sane. That is all I can hope right now,' I said to her as I laughed as well.

26

Miriam

'We are our own predators.'

An emergency at home! My father was in the Intensive Care Unit at Nairobi Hospital. My mother thought it was a heart attack — they were running a bunch of tests. He might have to be flown to the United States or South Africa if he worsened. *We the rich don't die in Kenya*, I couldn't help thinking. Either way, he would love to have his two sons by his side, and she wanted me to catch the first flight out. If he were to die before I got there, my mother would never forgive that I was busy chasing a story, and for *The National Inquisitor*. And I did want to go home and see him — the cold war with my parents could not continue. And while my future was with *The National Inquisitor*, I did want to do stories that I cared about, that mattered. An oxymoron to some — that one could write stories that matter for a tabloid, that I would want to become a serious tabloid journalist, but it is my medium; it is what I am good at.

And that is precisely why I could not leave yet — I had a few hours before the last flight. I did not want to think about the worst, the gut-wrenching pain I would feel if he passed away while I was in Addis, and the guilt. But I was where I was supposed to be for my story. And if I was where I was supposed to be, then the choice before me, to leave Addis or stay, had to be false.

In a strange way, it made me my father's son — his life was a singular pursuit of power and wealth, and mine was writing good stories. I lied to my mother, told her I would be catching the first flight out. She made me promise.

Maaza was downstairs at the hotel lobby waiting for me. Maaza and I, the self-appointed Bonnie and Clyde of Tizita, we said to hell with everything and made the journey to Miriam's village to talk to her cousin.

* * *

To visit the village where Miriam once lived was to be disabused of all that you knew about Ethiopia. Even I, who should have known better after visiting Kidane's rural home, was still shocked by the greenness of the highlands. Bob Geldof, and much later, Bono, had pulled a number on the world; they had redefined the image of a whole continent to one that was always holding a beggar's bowl — a black hand stretched out for blessings from a white hand — with the help of African leaders for whom suffering immediately translated into dollars and pounds.

Ethiopia had always been great for Kenyan nationalism. Yes, much had changed, and now Ethiopia rivalled Kenya and was even poised to beat it in the much-coveted race towards being the best wards of global capitalism. But national memory still retained the old Ethiopia of starving kids, the country's soundtrack stuck on the song "We Are the World." Ours was a national memory fed a steady diet of how much better off we were than our neighbours. Parents even today warn their kids not to waste their food because of the starving kids in Ethiopia. And, of course, during wedding parties, the drunken uncles and aunts reminded us that our Kenya was the land of milk and honey that was being sucked dry by the Ethiopians, Sudanese and Somalis.

So, the Ethiopian highlands and their abundance of deep healthy green, from grass to the coffee plantations, were, in spite of myself, a surprise. A deep, rich green going into the horizon, a Garden of Eden where the foliage is so thick that it seems like all you have to do is drop a seed and it sprouts right up before your eyes. Looking at this greenery, one understands why the Italians failed to conquer and colonise Ethiopia. No people would give this up without a struggle to the death.

Maaza could see my look of embarrassed confusion, but she merely shrugged it off as we drove up to a small wooden gate that opened up to Aamina Hakim's small compound. I imagined being Miriam and losing my family to famine and wars, to be that alone, and I could see why her cousin, the sole keeper of her memories, was important to her.

Call it a bias of youth, but I had always associated the word 'cousin' with someone young, and the first thing I noticed as Aamina welcomed us to her hut and started making tea was how old and frail she was.

Miriam had given me some things to bring to her — clothes,

shoes, a solar-powered mobile phone charger and some Kenyan tea and coffee. And, in true Miriam fashion, she had rigged one of the boxes so that a balloon popped out and burst. Instinctively, we fell to the ground, even old Aamina, and it was with much laughter that we dusted ourselves off.

'Yes, now I know Miriam sent you. She was always playing tricks on us, wrapping little pieces of soap like candy, covering cow pies with grass — oh, how our unsuspecting feet suffered! She was always up to no good. Doesn't surprise me she works as a bartender,' she said, laughing.

'You keep in touch?' Maaza asked.

'On and off over the years. I am glad she is finally doing some singing — what a waste of talent. It is never too late; as long as you are breathing, you can turn a life around.'

She talked really fast, like she was running out of time.

'She was singing as a child?' I followed up.

'Her and her sister — what wonderful voices! They knew pain from a young age; that is why when they sang, you could hear tears even in their most joyous songs. Their father, a farmer, was killed in the Ogaden. Her husband lost to the war. And then her sister died from AIDS—'

'AIDS? She told us she died fighting against the Eritreans?' I asked.

'We are a society of secrets — everything under lock and key. She suffered alone because no one spoke about it — shame and secrets. All the tragedies landed on their doorstep to spare the rest of us. And God has given us long lives so that we can live for those who died,' she said, clearly wanting to believe that was the case. It did not make sense any other way.

'Children?' I asked her.

'No, they had not got into it yet,' she said, winking at Maaza.

She asked me to help her with a trunk that was underneath her bed. She dug into it and emerged with some cassette tapes and letters and handed them over to me, pointing to a small, soot-darkened, formerly metallic-coloured tape player.

I picked one at random and played it. The first song was a duet — two kids singing "Silent Night," only they did not know the words but could mimic the lyrics. But some of the cassettes were not of children playing and recording themselves. Some of them were semi-professionally produced, and they were all of Miriam's sister. Pulling one of the cases open and looking at the credits, I found Miriam credited as one of the backup vocals singers.

On the tapes, I found only one Tizita song by her sister, but her voice was no longer the same; it sounded weak and old — ravaged by AIDS, Aamina explained. And that is where Miriam emerges from the background vocals, her sound so physical and alive that I could hear her helping her sister walk along, and her sister, being older, rejecting the help. And so Miriam walks not quite in the background and not alongside her. I hear her walking one step behind, propping up her stubborn sister every time she falters. Every now and then, they fall to the ground, and Miriam helps her up. And once she is up and walking, she slaps Miriam's hand away. Her sister, though she sounds frail, when held up by Miriam so that her remaining strength can go into the song, comes alive out of the old cassettes.

It made sense that there was no way of understanding Miriam outside of her sister. That talent — to have lived so close to it and in its shadow, to have recognised it as better than hers, and then for it to be lost, unrealised. To have watched that happen to a person she loved and looked up to, a person who had even helped define her own voice, would have come at a cost. That, compounded by the loss of her entire family, would have made the price exorbitant. It meant that she could not manage the intensity of her own life and the intensity demanded of her by the Tizita. It had to be one or the other, and she had chosen life over her gift.

After making us drink her tea, Aamina wrapped up Miriam's belongings in a small box and walked us to her doorway. As Maaza and I walked back to her car, she pointed up to a perfect moon, half shadow, half light. I saw it so clearly that I could feel the crunch of my boots on its rough surface.

'This Miriam of yours — that is some life. I hear that story every day at work, and each time I get angry. War and death — all of her pain has been caused by another human being, someone like her. That is what I can never understand — that we cause each other misery; rape, torture and murder each other. We are own predators,' she said, as we tried to process Miriam's story.

* * *

Maaza drove me to the airport so I could catch my last flight. She was beautiful, intelligent and passionate; she had my kind of sense of humour. If you added her good income, she was my ideal woman on paper, but there was nothing between us. It would have taken too much effort to fan the little sexual tension between us into a full-blown relationship. It felt right that we work and play together and be there for each other in the future. It was as if we both could anticipate crises in our future that would require that we help each other out and were saving our friendship for that. It could be that I had not yet recovered from The Diva's lesson at her juke joint, or from my rather poor performance at the orgy.

'Goodbye, my brother,' Maaza said as we hugged.

'I hope to see you soon, my sister,' I said. 'Thank you,' I added as we let go.

'Thank me by sending me the stories worth my effort, okay?' she said, and gave me her business card. I did the same.

'This is like we are becoming strangers, working our way backwards,' she said.

'My name is...,' I said, playing along.

'Good luck with everything,' she said, and playfully shoved me into the security line.

27

'I am ready to bring them back.'

I arrived at JKA to be immediately whisked to my father's bedside. No customs; my mother's driver literally met me by the plane. I asked him how my father was, but he did not reply. I asked him where my mother was, and he said he did not know. I understood enough to let it pass — the people who worked for my mother had no respect for me. In me, they saw an ingrate, and they knew they were more likely to rely on my brother for future employment when my parents passed. I called her, and she said she had just left the hospital, but I should go see him.

My father, it was now confirmed, had suffered a heart attack — no surprise there, really, given his daily Tusker and *nyama-choma* habit. He had just undergone open-heart surgery and was slipping in and out of consciousness. I placed my hand on his and looked around the hospital room. To make my father feel more at home, my mother had brought in some photographs; none of them were of her family. They were photos of them with the who's who of Kenya. She had accessorised the room in other ways: expensive curtains and a massive flat TV screen.

I was holding his hand, feeling sorry for him. Did he take secret pleasure in knowing that his wife had been fucking the most powerful man in the country? I did not want to imagine it, but I was angry enough to walk myself through porn videos I had watched — where the husband sits on the bed and watches as another man fucks his wife, holding the man's dick for his wife to suck and sometimes joining her in getting a facial. At some level, I could not help thinking, it could have been them playing out their sexual fantasies — power and sex rolled up in one. It could have just been that: three consenting adults in cuckold sexual fantasies, something they would have done anyway as professors or accountants.

I had once asked my brother whether he knew.

'Yes. But why the fuck do you care about our parents' sex life? That, to me, is what is so sick,' he had answered angrily. 'They have been good parents, no?' he had then asked more gently.

'Fuck no,' I said, and we both shared a rare laugh.

'I think what bothers me the most is that it is with someone who has ruined the country, killed people,' I had defended myself.

'We have never lacked for anything. Everything else is either none of your business or politics,' he tried to conclude for both of us.

All roads lead us to our deathbed, I thought as I leaned over to say goodbye, for the moment, to my father. He tried to will himself into full consciousness, but the drugs won, to my relief.

I left the hospital and went to *The National Inquisitor* bureau to report to Alison. She immediately wanted to know where I was with the story and for me to file my travel receipts. I explained that all I needed was to finish my write-up on Miriam and cover the final competition, which was in four days. But before then, Miriam was going to a wedding, and I was going to be her date.

* * *

It was a big wedding, one bringing two wealthy families, one Ethiopian and the other Kenyan, together. I had never met the bride or bridegroom, which was surprising to me — I prided myself on knowing the Nairobi wealthy and celebs. Wealth was on display — from the expensive cars to the decorations, to the outfits worn by everyone else besides Miriam and me, the odd couple for numerous obvious reasons. Miriam was dressed in a long, blue dress and red high heels that were a size or two bigger — she had shrunk, she swore. I was dressed in a white Ethiopian shirt with lions embroidered along the buttons, which I had bought at the airport. The symbolic nature of the union, two peoples, two cultures and two nations, was drummed into everything — from napkins with Ethiopian and Kenyan flags to our singing the two national anthems to kick off the ceremony.

Miriam knew the grandmother of the bride; they had formed a friendship on first arriving in Kenya and navigating the immigration mazes together. This she explained as we were being seated close to the high table. The wedding dragged on and on, as Kenyan weddings do. Politicians gave speeches, clergymen preached, uncles and aunts spoke, presents were given, or more aptly, donated — from a king-size bed to pots and pans to a brand-new Peugeot from the parents. People starved, children cried, one or two old people fainted — but finally we ate, the taps to alcohol were opened, a wedding band started playing the usual standards — "Malaika," Houston's "I Will Always Love You," and, of course, "Islands in the Stream" by Kenny Rogers and Dolly Parton.

By early evening, the wedding was now a raging party, and Miriam was having fun dancing and drinking with her old friend, while I sampled the various whiskies. At some point, her friend went to the microphone and said she had a special gift to the married couple — a Tizita by one of the best but unknown singers of her generation.

'The bitch ambushed me,' Miriam happily whispered to me.

'You can use the practice; the competition is in two days,' I said in solidarity.

As she got on stage and started singing, trying to get the band into the right key and rhythm, I knew it was going to be a failed performance, and I started to dread the carnage. For one, the saxophonist was playing off key. The guitarist, we couldn't even hear. There were too many false starts, notes helter-skelter. They would seem to get on the same groove, then something would happen, and they would come undone. But the wedding crowd loved it. It was a gift in the deepest sense of the word — an artist put on the spot, on stage, warts and all; to see the music being made.

A blind man playfully yelled that he was going to rescue his lovely Miriam and tapped his way onto the stage with one hand, the other carrying an expensive-looking krar.

'Ladies and gentlemen...Gabriel Afsaw!' Miriam announced him.

The Ethiopians recognised him because they yelled out his name and crowded the stage to hear him. He set up shop as the rest of the band quieted down and, as if on a volume dial, his krar and Miriam's voice came up to the forefront. The more I listened to his krar and her voice, the more I could not help feeling that he was seeing, blind as he was, something in its barest essence — sound, perhaps? Sensing sound? An image for an artist, would it not be a sensation? A feeling?

The band came back in. The saxophonist had given up his sax for a harmonica, and he was breathing in and out a jagged wailing sound, then showing off in a loving way that he could dig even deeper by drawing a sound so long and varied he ran out of air and took long, painful breaths — as if to say, *Only by dying a little can you play the perfect note.*

If I did not know any better, I would have sworn that Miriam and the blind man were lovers. The sound of the blind man's krar against the harmonica — he was snapping the strings so fast that it felt like sound had become a physical entity, pushing out wave after wave. Miriam's singing and his krar were in a heated debate, like one between cheating lovers, the sex that comes from a pathological relationship. So they argued, threatened fire and brimstone, dug into each other's old wounds; they laughed and loved together. Sometimes the drummer wanted to hug them and calm them down, and other times he would threaten and shout at them. And the harmonica kept digging them out of their quarrelsome world to remind them of the love they had lost, or risked losing, or were making.

Miriam's voice. At the end of each phrase, I could hear it. There was a rasp, sometimes empty air, like she had spit close to the mic, rapidly flicked her tongue so that her voice also became breath that became sound. A contained roar, a roar of rage, love — any two extreme emotions — what would that sound like? The answer was the voice we were listening to, somewhere between the wail of 'someone has died,' and the wail of 'someone has been born.' What could be better than for that wail to be expressed by multiple voices and instruments? An orchestra on stage? Or just a single, solitary krar? The answer was in her voice, which, to my ear, contained many voices, like someone possessed by a choir. Like Kidane's voice, only hers was older.

And then her voice rose, high and fast, and for a moment, she lost the blind man. She waited, tapping her foot, swaying, until he caught up with her. Her old voice rose yet again — soft and hard, resolute but searching — above the testosterone-driven krar, sax and drums. This voice in sound and not words was asking all of us to have a little more fun, just kick back.

At times, she would fall behind and playfully skip along until she caught up to the band, and then she would soar again. She was flailing her arms, but there was a pattern — her hands were playing, or dancing, or even imagining something I could not quite understand until I thought of her dead sister. And then it made sense; her hands were singing her dead sister's parts, filling in and giving life to her dead, absent voice.

The blind man, it seemed to me, had uncovered the secret to the krar. The krar, this four-stringed instrument with no frets to change keys and tone, was not for dazzling slides up and down a scale or for Jimi Hendrix play-with-your-teeth-then-burn-the-guitar kind of antics. The krar with its four strings — what you see is what you get. But that does not make it a simple instrument. Hold a krar in your arms, these four strings, and they will remain mute, even in their simplicity, unless you know. The secret had something to do with speed, timing and suggestion — all of them one and the same thing.

She — they — had conquered the audience. Everyone was dancing slow, holding tight to someone. I was missing something in me — love, perhaps, or my other lives — very badly. The song came to an end, and a triumphant Miriam came back to our table.

'I am ready,' she said as I hugged her.

'Your sister and your family...?' I asked her, wanting her story then, with the Tizita still floating around us.

'Tell me more, but do not depress me in a fucking wedding,' she answered.

I felt my heart flutter as I doubted my ability to tell her story — was I a voyeur, slumming her story for my tabloid?

'Tell me about singing with your sister. I listened to your recordings, your tapes,' I said, knowing what I wanted — and selfishly — was to feel her story, what Jack and I never had.

We were now sitting next to each other, alone in a wedding.

'You found her — you needed to find her,' she said. 'I hoped you would — the gift of memory. I can remember because you asked.'

'Singing with her?'

Miriam looked up. 'It was heaven. I hope you find that, to be in heaven with someone while on earth.' She took a sip from her drink.

I did not say anything.

'It's not memory. This is what the Tizita is telling you: "I am ready to bring them back." Tizita is a memory that is as alive as you and I now. I will bring them back,' she said and waltzed off with her friend, back to the dance floor.

28

*'Ask anything — but you have to
really ask it, if I am to answer.'*

I was at the hospital, visiting my father. He had just come out of a morphine-induced sleep long enough to call me Jack before correcting himself. I wanted to tell him that his beloved Jack was abroad making money, but instead I watched silently as he drifted back into disappointed unconsciousness. My mother tried to console me. And it was then that I was seized by anger — it was time to ask about the dictator, my name and whatever else I was going to be able to dredge up.

'Listen, Ma, I have to ask you something,' I said to her as I sat up straight.

She tensed up. 'Ask anything — but you have to really ask it, if I am to answer,' she said.

And right at that moment when I could have asked anything — the dictator, my name, her relationship with my father, the choices they had made for themselves and my brother and me at the expense of thousands of others — right at that moment when I could have asked anything, and I believe she would have answered honestly, I realised how little any of it mattered.

None of it mattered. My parents were never going to change; they had watched the growing democracy movement, and it had not changed them. In fact, they had warned us against being involved in anti-government strikes, and to my shame, I had listened. Democracy came, and they still bribe their way through anything. Democracy came and left them still wealthy and powerful. They were who they were, and they would change only when the circumstances that had created them changed.

And I was never going to love them any less. I was not a saint, neither were those around me — far from it, in fact. And working for the dictator, or cuckolding with him, that was their choice, not mine. I did not have to inherit their shit, so to speak. I was just in an orgy, for fuck's sake. Yes, I was marked by their choices, as we all are by the choices our parents make for themselves, but I did not have to inherit their guilt. Maybe I just did not want to look too closely at my own life and choices. What I needed to do was figure out my own life.

'Listen, Ma, when Dad is feeling well, I want to tell you about my trip to Ethiopia,' I said, instead of asking all the questions pent up inside me about them.

She gasped, in relief perhaps, and grasped my hand. Right at that moment, my father willed himself into the conversation. He painfully pulled himself up and asked my mother to leave us. She wanted to protest, but something about the way they looked at each other reminded me of those days when they would exchange looks that said it was time to implement whatever agenda they had agreed upon. And so she left, and I sat down and pulled my chair closer to him.

'Manfredi, really ask what you want to ask. If I die — I could have died....'

I leaned in closer. 'It's okay. It no longer matters. Ethiopia was really good for me,' I said, trying to stop the conversation that was about to happen from taking place.

'The 2,000 dollars...,' he started to say but caught himself. 'I could have died. And then where would you be? If something is not said, it still matters. If you leave this room without asking what you want to ask, then the rest of your life is on you,' he said, sounding more like my father from a distant past, when his love for his children, for me, was visceral.

I felt angry. I wanted to hurt him. 'Since you insist, then I must. Did you know the dictator was fucking your wife? You must have known; you went with her there, even took us along. Did you like watching?' I asked him, surprising myself at the words I was using.

I felt relief, then fear that I had damaged our relationship beyond repair. And best and worst of all, I welcomed a panicked feeling of superiority. That startled him. He reflexively tried to hit me, but the tubes that were giving him morphine and other liquids held him back. He leaned into his raised bed in pain. Several emotions radiated from him, and I could read each one of them — shame, a flash of voyeuristic pleasure, anger and then indignation. And then one I could not see coming, could never have seen coming — humour. He started laughing.

'Well, son, when I said you could ask, that was not what I had in mind,' he said.

I started to laugh too, but he started coughing.

I filled a glass with water and gave it to him. His hands trembled, and I held the glass of water to his lips. He sipped, leaned back and composed himself, back to the father I knew. He reached out a sickly, tired arm ridden with IV tubes and valves and placed it on my shoulder.

'Son, I love your mother. I love her more than my own life, or even yours or that of your brother.'

'Is he really my brother? Am I truly your biological son?' I asked, now that I had found an opening. The answer did not really matter — I was not going to go around claiming my dictatorship heritage. And, in truth, while I entertained the thought to drive myself mad, I never thought it could be true, deep down. It's not like male infidelity matters politically — dictators love their property, especially if boys, and I am sure he would have come collecting. But still....

He leaned back onto the bed, turned his head so that he was looking right at me.

'Yes, you are. That has never been in doubt.... But what I am trying to tell you is that we put too much premium on sex; sex is not an expression of love; sex is for pleasure, and she can get it from someone else. Why would I stop her? You know what they say — the vagina is not like soap that gets finished, neither is the penis,' he added lightly but seriously.

'But that is not just it. You supported the dictator. He was killing people, and you did nothing. You profited. You let him fuck my mother and kill people so both of you could profit,' I said, feeling the words come out of me in spite of myself.

'Yet you take our money, no? You are a grown man, and yet you take our money. Why, if it's that bloody?' he asked.

'So now you are blaming me?' I threw the question at him.

'No, I am just pointing out your hypocrisy. If you truly believed what you just said, you would not take a single shilling from us. What I am trying to tell you is that there are no answers for your life here,' he answered, sounding like a father. 'But you, you have lived your life. There are no answers for your life here,' he tried to clarify. I did not know what to say, so I kept quiet.

Of all the people who should have understood the Tizita, it was my parents. The anguish that is love, the love that is selfish, the love that can create life and watch others die, that is itself. Somewhere between the pragmatism of needing power and money to survive and being married, my parents were one fucked-up Tizita. But precisely because they took so much life from others, they could hear the Tizita without really listening to it.

'It is just sex. Surely, you are old enough to understand that,' he said, and I could feel him watching me, trying to gauge my reaction.

'Did you ever fuck the president's wife?' I asked, to his laughter.

'No. I only....'

In that second, in slow motion, I wondered what was coming next after the 'only,' what other possibilities — I only watched, jerked off, cried, laughed, fucked other women, the president's sister, maid and so on.

And then he said it. 'I only fucked the president.'

We laughed so hard that I started worrying about his health — death from laughter would have made a nice headline at the *Inquisitor*.

'Son, I am not joking. Think about that every time you see him on TV.'

It did not change the politics or the extent to which the ruling class had fucked up Kenya, but still, what a thought! He was fucking the dictator while the dictator was fucking my mother. All in all, I think he had a point; we put too much premium on sex.

It was good to finally talk.

I had to make it to the ABC for the final competition. I told him I had to rush off, and he asked me if I could come back in the morning.

'It might be a late night,' I said to him.

He tried to wink.

I stepped outside the hospital room. My mother was standing out in the hallway, her hands rubbing her belly like she was in pain.

'Are you okay?' I asked.

'Yeah, yeah, I am fine. How did it go?' she asked.

'Well, it was good to finally talk,' I said, trying to answer a question that she had not verbalised.

'All I want for you is to be happy...every now and then,' she said.

'I have to go, but I will be back as soon as I can,' I said.

'You mean that? That you will be back?' she asked.

'Of course, Ma — can we not do this? Of course, I mean it,' I said to her, beginning to doubt myself just a little bit.

'Wait!' she whispered urgently.

I stopped.

'I love your father. I have always loved your father,' she said.

'Maybe then you should not have been...,' I started to say but checked myself when I saw the look of pity start to cross her face, the kind you give a child you have unavoidably hurt.

'Well, maybe he needs to hear that,' I said and smiled at her, conscious of just how little over the years I had shown any affection for her.

She shook her head from side to side, smiling. We hugged, and I was off to the ABC.

29

'Tizita, how will I caress my lover with these hands
That killed her brother, or sister or father
Or mother, Tizita, Tizita, Tizita...'

Like the last time, the ABC crowd was a mixture of Ethiopians and Kenyans (from the slummers to those who were being slummed) busy talking about music and who would win. It was a hot night, and people had come up with all sorts of ingenious ways to keep cool, like placing the cold beer on their foreheads or fanning themselves with money before handing it to the bookies. There were a thousand and one stories in here waiting for me.

I was sitting at the counter, looking over my notes, wondering what happened to the story I wanted to write. It was as if instead of writing about a hurricane, I had been drawn inside one, and I was fighting for my very own survival. Now that my Tizita journey was almost over, I had some fast thinking to do about what I was going to do next.

I had not seen The Diva/Kidane or the other musicians, except for Miriam, for a few weeks, and I was anxiously excited, like I was waiting to see old dear friends and ex-lovers. This time, Miriam was not at the bar; she was busy getting ready in the back. Mr. Selassie had hired a temporary bartender whom he kept watching to make sure he was not pocketing some of the money.

I was realising some things, or rather, they were floating to where I was standing, with my feet planted in this lake, or ocean, of life. What attracted me to places like the ABC, and why I had not amounted to much, why I was never going to win the Kenya journalist of the year award or the CNN Africa journalist of the year, was because what I loved doing the most was writing about the weird, that which exists just outside the edges of what we want to know. The weird, but not so terribly weird that it becomes newsworthy and trendy.

I was drawn to writing about the crazy old guy who wore nylon sisal sacks and nothing else, even though he could have worn clothes donated to him by a local church or walked about naked with his crazy licence. He would wear only sisal sacks. He just felt more comfortable in sacks, he would say when asked. I should write his story.

Or this other guy who had been a newscaster before madness caught up with him — and now he sits in a bar in my hometown, where he reads newspapers as if on TV for free beer and food. I had told Maaza the story, imitating the crazily groomed, moustache-twisted-at-the-end, fast-talking crazy newscaster with the uncombed, dreading afro. I should write his story.

Or get this about the Kikuyu. Traditionally, women could marry women. One of the women had to be propertied, preferably be a widow, before being allowed to marry another woman. Some women had multiple wives. When I was growing up, a neighbour to one of my relatives was married to a woman. Everyone wanted to believe the marriages were asexual, but common sense would suggest otherwise. I should write about it; it would be perfect for *The National Inquisitor*. Why should I care about digging dirt in the city sewers when I could write about lesbian sex and marriage amongst the Kikuyu? Life itself was a tabloid!

Mr. Selassie got on the mic and thanked all of us for coming. With fanfare, he opened a briefcase. 'Five million Kenya shillings in dollars,' he announced. He could have said, 'Fifty thousand or so dollars,' but it would not have had the same ring to it; the purse in dollars would have felt lighter. He called up one of his bouncers to come and hold up a boxing championship belt that read in big gold letters 'King of Tizita.'

'Queen!' the audience yelled, almost in unison.

'A king is also queen,' Mr Selassie said, trying to get away with it. More boos.

'The rules are,' Mr. Selassie paused for maximum effect and yelled, 'there are no rules!'

A roar of approval followed.

'Except one,' he added. The crowd jeered him.

'On the pain of death, there will be no recording,' he finished.

No one at the ABC would break that rule, unless it was someone who did not know Mr. Selassie.

'May the best man or woman win!'

And with that, the competition started.

The Taliban Man

The Taliban Man walked briskly towards the stage, stopping two or three times to bow to the near-hysterical crowd. He was dressed in a business suit, his hair braided and pulled back into a ponytail. He was in sharp contrast to the humble and chaotic ABC; he was a walking island of perfectibility — youth, looks and self-possession all rolled into one. He waved as he jumped into the boxing ring stage, walked to his guitar, raised it up for all to see and kissed it.

He said he was going to warm us up first by doing a version of his "Taliban Man's Song," but this time in Amharic and rapping only the chorus (which he had tweaked since the last time I heard it) in English. By the time he was doing the chorus a third time, the crowd was ready to join in, missing some of the words but not the spirit of the song — a coliseum of voices rapping, some falling out and others joining:

The Taliban Man is here to stay
But my love is always ahead of me
I follow her, and we drink and love
From the river of this life, in hell or heaven
You strike a child, you strike The Taliban Man
Strike me and you have struck my woman

He waited for our laughter to subside. 'Now you are ready…. This Tizita is by the lovely Bezawork,' he said as he adjusted and clasped his capo onto the guitar's neck. He strummed once or twice to make sure it was still in tune and got to it.

He slipped into Bezawork's Tizita, with echoes of The Diva's rendition in front of 60,000 people back in Addis still ringing in my ears.

One would have expected the bravado of hip-hop to carry through into his music, but his voice sounded like it was straining against a hammer that was beating it down at every note as it tried to soar alongside his guitar. And yet, maybe because what we could hear was his vulnerability as his voice searched for something it could not quite get to, it was beautiful. He was still not quite there.

He slid the capo up, narrowed down the distance between sounds, his fingers moving so furiously that time came to a standstill, and then he let his voice rush into the slowed-down waterfall.

And that was when I heard it, his singing at the end of what he knew, his singing so that he would not get overwhelmed by the knowledge of what he did not know. It was, in its own way, a vulnerability that had taken control. Was he questioning, reaching out to God or to love or to death? If you could sing from the point where you could see something, something so real you know is there and yet unknowable, would you not sound like The Taliban Man? And if you could sustain that over a whole song, would that be a mastery of how to speak about that which you cannot really know? Listening to The Taliban Man, I sensed death, and I sensed life, and I was okay with either. I thought The Taliban Man would win — his Tizita was life and the fear and the love of what would come next. A young man singing into a future that he and all of us could only touch with our fingertips, constantly moving forward, out of reach. He was singing the vague awareness of transition.

Then he jumped into that transition to make sense of it for us. And his sound — he had found it — I had to tease it out, and perhaps it was lost on the crowd, but it was there, and it was getting bolder and bolder — and it was mine to hear. He was thumbing the bass string so that it suggested the familiar Tizita bass as he was picking the strings; his left was picking them too, hammering down on them and picking them, his right hand picking, his left hammering and bending. It was as if he was playing the krar, only the guitar rounded off the notes in a way the krar could not. The sound that came out was somewhere between Malian blues and Lingala, and yet it was Ethiopian. He had found the boldness of hip-hop and the vulnerability of the blues. There was no mimicry — he tapped into the river of all sound; and all sound, like all languages, speak in notes and meter. These were his languages. He had found his sound — Ethiopia, Africa and the world would be hearing of him soon, I thought.

As he was walking off the stage, I suddenly glimpsed an old man, guitar slung over his shoulder like it was a shovel — like he had quickly shape-shifted before reverting back to The Taliban Man. Is this what The Diva had seen and heard in him?

I texted Maaza, *I think your brother has found it. He will take it home tonight.*

She texted right back, *Patience, young grasshopper!*

I was sure of one thing, I would regret the rest of my life

because I would never see the kind of beauty this night was promising. No one can be that lucky.

Miriam

Miriam playing the sax? Impossible! And yet...I was sitting close enough to hear the metallic tapping of the keys and an intensely painful staccato of wails — high and then so low that I could hear her reaching deep down enough to hold the devil's hand. Who was she missing? Her sister or the corporals? Her aunt?

Miriam on the saxophone, her bony chest in a red silk slip heaving rapidly — I was afraid she was going to die on stage. Exhausted, she put the sax down and laughed into the mic as if to say, *See what I could do in my younger days?* As beautiful as it was, I was relieved when she picked up the krar as we cheered her on.

Listening to her and the krar, it struck me — what if all along I had it wrong? What if the singer was not trying to outshine the guitar, the piano, the strings or the krar? That it was in fact the other way around, and it was the instrument in competition with the human voice? It was the instruments trying to match the human voice, and that bravado we hear in solos was their attempt at taking centre stage? Miriam's voice was showing the krar its limitations, and rather than out-sing it, she was finding harmony with it, and then leading it along.

Why did we create the guitar, the masenko, the saxophone and the krar? To take meaning, words out of sound, I thought. The human voice matters to us only to the extent it says or sings words. And even when we cannot hear or understand the words, we still find comfort in that in there is some decipherable meaning, if only we spoke the language. We wanted the human voice to do the work of meaning, so we invented the musical instruments to take the place of the human voice as a musical instrument — to be sound. And all along we have been trying to answer the question, what is sound? The instruments can create sound, but they cannot tell us what it is.

Listening to the Tizita in a language I did not speak or understand, I could hear Miriam's voice as an instrument doing the beautiful work of voice and instrument. I could hear the human voice as an instrument in concert with other instruments, in love and at war, all at the same time. This tension was what broke Miriam's voice into several sounds, guttural and refined, coarse, rough, unsure, human and disembodied, vulnerable to imperfection and yet able to soar like the saxophone she had been playing. To hear Miriam's voice as sound and instrument was to hear the human voice as God intended it — something to always remind us that we are human beings to each other; our voices were not meant to order executions and bombings, wars and genocides. The original sound, the sound of a human voice, is a reminder of the love that binds us, as death awaits us all in the end anyway. Language as sound is the inheritance each generation passes on to the next, from Miriam to The Diva to The Taliban Man.

Every now and then Miriam would challenge the krar, and they would both climb up a mountain, and when the krar tiredly started lagging behind, she would wait, impatiently —

a sweet, deep anticipation that became tension would fill the room. That tension, that is the krar's gift to the singer who does not try to out-sing it; the krar trains the singer to find and create tension. If the krar's sound was a straight line, train tracks with missing rails every few meters, Miriam's voice was making a million tiny waves along, underneath and above them.

What Miriam was telling us, like James Baldwin had, was that we live in our times; we cannot live outside of them, but she was adding that we can dance just ever so slightly above this finite rhythm that is our lives. That tension — it was like peering into the inside of a grenade.

Looking at Miriam, I wondered how she could get by on stage with so little movement, subtle movements that seemed to magnify her voice, make her frail body seem stronger, subtle little movements that seemed to send a wave, another wave and another one, each amplifying the music separating each instrument from the other, and her voice somewhere — her body, like the body of a guitar, part of an instrument. Everything about her, literally everything about her while she was on stage, was about sound and music.

And she was singing using a language, with words — but each word was a burst of wind, riding on the repetitiveness of the krar, sometimes wrapping itself around the bass string, sometimes tapping alongside the beat — and then just like that, she was gone. And I followed the krar into her world. There, I too was just sound, awkwardly tall and wordy in speech, I was sound that could not wrap around the beats and her voice. I jumped in and let myself fall, no safety net, nothing — and she caught me. I was falling, and I held on to her voice. I heard her teaching me how to listen, not just listening to learn, but to be one with other people — and the whole ABC vibrated along, our hands held together by the Tizita, our feet dipped in a common pool of tears, our happiness all around us.

She was done. She was met with a stunned silence, but when it broke into applause, it threatened to tear down the ABC. I went to the stage to help her down.

'You did bring them back,' I said to her, remembering what she had told me at the wedding.

'Thanks, babe,' was all she said in reply.

The Corporal

On stage, The Corporal was sitting on a three-legged stool, wearing a striped black jacket on top of a dirty brownish shirt that was once white, a cheap red tie, the legs of his blue pants pulled up to his ankles to reveal blue striped socks; his chin lay on hands resting on the masenko, a tired but calm face, almost hidden by a feathered fedora. If it were not for the way he was dressed, he would have looked like any worker on a farm, leaning tiredly on a hoe to rest, or a soldier resting his arm on the barrel of an AK-47. There was something about the way he sat there that told me music was a necessary chore for him, work he did in spite of himself.

I rushed over to Mr. Selassie and blurted, 'You have to tell me....'

'Tell me?' he asked.

'I mean, translate — words,' I corrected myself.

He thought for a moment. 'Only for you, Doc. You have earned it,' he said with his laugh. He might have meant that my earlier doctored piece had brought in a larger crowd, or I had been working hard on the Tizita. Either way, I did not care. What I cared about was whether he would dare do a simultaneous translation. My plan was to get the raw stuff from him and work on it later.

'He says he is going to sing a new Tizita; in English, it means, life in a life.' And so, The Corporal went to work, with Mr. Selassie translating as I took notes and recorded. For the title, I wrote down "Life within a Life"; later, it would become "Two Lives in One." But Mr. Selassie's spontaneous translation and the spirit of the night would be the keys that mattered.

My voice, my tongue, my memory, my whole being
I find myself dropping like a stone weighed by the moss
It has gathered, collected as I rolled through life faster
Than a bullet, Tizita, Tizita, Tizita, Tizita, Tizita
Tizita, how will I caress my lover with these hands
That killed her brother, or sister or father
Or mother, Tizita, Tizita, Tizita,

His was an interesting style of singing the Tizita, ending each line with such a smooth finality that it sounded like an experienced hand with a machete cutting through sugar cane. And yet, the words of his Tizita were asking questions of his life and our lives.

Oh, Tizita — I should know, because I once went to war
To find myself, but what I found I cannot reconcile
With what I wanted to remember, a time when

We were one, wading deep in rivers of love,
In the war I waded deep in another kind
Of love with a name I cannot say

He bowed the masenko long and hard; I could feel the weight of whatever it was he could not say. As he pulled back the bow, there was a collective gasp of awe at this sound that was both devil and god, that threatened to swallow them both into this lone human's masenko, who out of sound wanted to create light.

I invoke you, Tizita, I beg/plead/kneel down
To take my memories so I can wake up tomorrow/day after
Back/in past of/ in time in a future where we have not learnt

The beautiful art of war, Tizita, oh, Tizita, Tizita
Tizita, how will I caress my lover with these hands
That killed her brother, or sister or father
Or mother, Tizita, Tizita, Tizita,

The masenko emphasised. At this point, especially with Mr. Selassie's voice breaking as he translated as if he could not do it fast enough, I was worried about what would follow next.

I do not want this love you have found for me
I do not want this love I have found in me,
Tizita, Tizita, oh, Tizita
Let me go back and die in that battlefield
A thousand times
Let me sink like a stone weighed down by the moss
It has gathered, deep down into the Nile

He was no longer singing, and his masenko had gone quiet. He spoke the words, as if a poem that still wanted to be sung.

Oh, Tizita — will I find warmth in the cold waters of the Nile?
Oh, Tizita, will I find light in the dark cold waters of my sins?
Tizita, Tizita, do not come with, here, even though we cannot
Must we just part ways, we have....

He stopped, ended his performance abruptly, his head bowed down. 'I am very sorry. The Tizita is not to be so raw — so fresh, not at all...,' he said.

He was done. I had heard of the Tizita described as being like the wind — you can tame it, use it to run your windmills or to set sail, but you could never truly own it.

To others, the Tizita was like a river, the same but never the same, constantly moving, new and old at the same time — a cliché that was new each time. And you ran the risk of someday being swallowed by something that was constantly in motion. To The Corporal, the Tizita was where he emptied his life, and this time it was heavy, just too fucking heavy.

Broken, he stopped playing and left the stage. We were not sure what to do, and we looked at each other for signs — is it okay to cry, or laugh? We settled on *he tried. Only a man can try that hard; sometimes to try is to win and so on*, we said to each other with our eyes.

Mr. Selassie rushed to the stage and announced The Diva.

The Diva/Kidane

What was The Diva going to do? Would she just glide along her glittery image before going back home, a lesser musician perhaps, but one who had not failed, at the very least? Or would she perform as Kidane? Would it matter if the truth of the Tizita was told by either? I did not have long to wait.

It was Kidane walking towards the stage, her hair cropped short; no long, looping ivory earrings; no long dress studded with diamonds (fake or real) drooping over her shoulders — just her in simple white Bata sneakers, wrapped in a *shuka*, the single sheet of sunflower-patterned wrap with an embroidered Kiswahili proverb: '*Akili ni nywele, kila mtu ana zake.*' I was not sure what to make of the proverb — that a brain is like hair, every human being has theirs — in this setting, but I imagined if she could have walked on stage naked, she would have. Her understated look had the men and women in the ABC talking in animated buzzing sounds.

Mustafa was behind her, but if you did not know him, you could not tell he was there to protect her. He was dressed down, like any overly branded 40-year-old American still hanging on to his youth: a 49ers football jersey, jeans, white Jordan Nikes and a Red Sox cap put on backwards.

Kidane walked over to the keyboard piano, bowed ever so lightly, waved to us, then sat down. She made some adjustments, took a deep breath, lifted her hands up and plunged in. Only it was not a plunge, it was like a long plaintive wail. She had set the keyboard to a church organ sound, and the wail, which was getting higher and higher, was being pulled back by the trembling black keys that gave a cascading bass line until she found a place for them to be in contentious harmony. And the way she found it was by throwing her voice at the overpowering church organ. And then she guided her voice in and out until she found a safe flight path through the turbulence of a church organ at war with itself.

She started humming along. She had so much control of her voice that it sounded like it was gushing out of a water faucet, from torrent to a steady pour to trickles to droplets, sometimes a mixture of torrent and droplet, or trickle and torrent. Then it hit me, her voice was like the sound pushed out of an accordion — pulled and squeezed, sweetness and bitterness, longing and hope, hope and hopelessness, longing and death, longing and life, longing and then the echoes of a stopped heartbeat.

Her voice always filling space like the church organ — a sound bigger than itself. To put it another way, imagine the sound of the proverbial bird that flies with the waves of a turbulent ocean — and the sand bed and the full moon that gives it its ebb and flow — imagine that bird singing inside, within and above the roaring ocean. That was what Kidane was able to do, her Tizita the bird working steadily, sometimes faltering, sometimes daring, through the storm created by the organ.

'By the way, this is a brand new Tizita,' she whispered into the microphone. We dug deeper into a silence that was the loudest applause I had ever heard. Kidane continued fanning the organ into sound.

She looked over at where The Taliban Man was sitting, drink in hand, looking cool as fuck. Their eyes locked; he dropped his drink on the table and half ran to the stage. Once settled in, he started something slow and intricate on the krar. She smiled at him but shook her head no. He tried something else — a classical Tizita on a clean, muted guitar — she shook her head no again. He started another tune, plucking at the bass and picking the higher strings, like the sound of different clocks striking midday at the same time, different yet the same. She threw her head back and laughed.

They had something. Was this how she was going to bring him in from the cold?

The Taliban Man jammed solo over her organ for a while before beckoning the broken Corporal, and he rushed to the stage armed with his masenko. He did not waste any time — he kept a steady, urgent beat, so that it sounded like the devil was chanting behind Kidane's organ. God and the devil duelling through sound as he chanted a devil's prayer, and Kidane stretched the sound of the organ.

The piano's many voices are within the multiple keys, within the instrument itself. The krar or the masenko — the instrument knows its weakness, understands it and does not try to mask it. It thrives to the extent it makes the listener do its work —

emotion has an infinite number of notes and strings, and a krar or masenko musician is as good as they can hit the notes within the listener; that is the genius of simplicity. Classical music, if you listen hard enough, works with that core, which it then masks with the orchestra; the krar and the masenko have no masks, save for the one the listeners, to their loss, might choose to wear.

Imagine jazz without improvisation, and yet it was demanded of it that it convey the same sense of adventure, the same intensity, like crying without tears, laughing without sound; what if it was demanded that the most intense of feelings be contained within a single phrase that never rose to the skies, that a whole poem be expressed in a syllable, one sound — what would that do to your voice and your instinct to celebrate by excess? If all you would do within this form was to contain your voice, and your voice was rebelling against the constraint because all you wanted was to break out, it would be like driving a sports car using the first gear, the engine pushing for speed and yet held back by something that was part of it. It would destroy it. Unless the Tizita musician learns how to contain that tension of a form that holds back flight...implosion, the grenade turned on itself — I now knew that was what had happened with The Corporal's failed new Tizita.

The Corporal's masenko tickled Kidane, and she laughed her snort-filled laugh, a freed laugh that became part of the music. She gestured at her bandmates to say thank you. And then, when she found an opening after a few minutes, she started singing, as Mr. Selassie translated into my ear, sometimes pulling it, to my irritation. 'By the way, this is a new Tizita,' she repeated.

> *I see a woman out in the mist of the waterfall*
> *She spins and spins and spins her Tizita*
> *But her Tizita was here and now it's gone and she spins*

Here, my trusty translator gave several versions of 'spins': 'out of control,' 'turns around really fast,' 'creates, as in spinning a world,' and he would have continued, but we were pulled back in by Kidane.

> *Naked but dressed by moving mist*
> *I used to stand by the waterfall and let the water*
> *Keep me warm, keep me warm and hold me*

> *I am standing balancing between being*
> *Born and dying, crazy, but to be born is to live*
> *And to die at the same time, but the Tizita,*

> *The Tizita, this Tizita — my lover yesterday*
> *This Tizita keeps me spinning by the waterfall, naked*
> *But dressed in an armour of silvery mist*

I could imagine this violent water, in Victoria Falls for example, hitting its bed and rocks, and me standing there, naked, feeling alive and terrified at the same time.

This water moves, this water finds more water
Down the steep hill and into an ocean. I hurled
Myself into the ocean, hurled myself into the ocean

And I swam in God's salty tears, and every time it rained
I knew God's sorrow, God's love had flooded the
Heaven gates overflowing into my Tizita

Ocean or river? Poured or rained? Threw, hurled or gave myself into the river? My translator threw all of them at me, but I ignored him and the multiple directions. Instead, I listened to The Corporal with his masenko — his violent energy, anger and terror coming to you as a fine, titillating cold mist that envelopes you; imagine that now coming at you as a voice singing this Tizita. Imagine an erupting volcano with all its terror, but now contained and squeezed through the one-stringed masenko.

Tizita, Tizita, I will keep dying so that I can live,
Tizita, Tizita, this song of many loves in the past,
And many loves to come, Tizita, the only river

They called Miriam to the stage. She got to the ring and started looking around. I walked over and helped her onto the stage. I rushed back to Mr. Selassie. And then, in a gesture that made the whole ABC tear up, Miriam sang The Corporal's last verse from his failed Tizita in a fierce and protective way.

Oh, Tizita, will I find warmth in the cold waters of the Nile?
Oh, Tizita, will I find light in the dark cold waters of my sins?

Tizita, Tizita, do not come with, here, even though we cannot
Must part ways, I am drowning, I cannot breathe

And then The Diva came in:

Tizita

Tizita

Tizita

A trickle of rain — last drop hanging on, water drop on icicle, last drop the suspense, hanging — this was the distance between the letting go of the wet, cold drop and the muted yet enunciated splash of the heavy, rushing drop hitting the wet ground. Trickle of rain — last drop hanging on, water sweating on icicle; last drop — hanging, that long, slow release and the rush to the ground. And they all came in with everything they had, instruments and voices, a slow rush to give an open conclusion.

Tizita

Tizita

Tizita

Tizita, Tizita, Tizita — each time, the same word sounded different. The first time, it sounded like they were asking the Tizita to come; there was some longing, some welcoming a broken heart because it still knew what love was. The second time, it sounded more like the distant beckoning of something soon to be lost — a memory of a loved one, details and memories getting lost in the distance of living with the dead behind us. The third time, it was a yearning, an unresolved recognition of something. In all the three invocations, the word — really, a phrase — went just beyond the form, yet the Tizita managed to pull it back. I couldn't say what Tizita was, but I finally knew it; I had felt it. I knew it, and yet the hunger hungered on, both complete and broken.

It was perfect — they were not gladiators and, more than that, it was the music that counted, and we could not have asked for a better grand finale. We, the audience-participants, the perhaps manipulated but malnourished faithful, we had won too.

I was going to take all the devils I had found in me, all that was in me, and I was going to make them fight and rage. But for what, though? Something in me, in all of us, had irrevocably shifted; yes, certainly for better and worse, because the slummers might not know what to do with feeling raw emotions, but we were not who we were just a few hours ago. Messy, but it was movement nevertheless.

Logically, I knew no one could script such an ending — it was as spontaneous as they come. It was a group of musicians who, even though speaking different languages of music, were true enough to grope their way to each other, sure that when they found each other, each throwing in a sliver that might clash with others, beauty would be theirs — a bunch of geniuses open to each other for that moment. And we got to listen, not just to listen, but to be recreated.

Mr. Selassie, my translator, was holding his head in his hands, and I put my arm around his shoulders.

'Doctor, translating for you, I experience the Tizita two times. I am a much poorer man — but I am also a much richer man,' he said. Then, looking up at me, he asked soberly, concerned, 'How are you going to write about this?'

'Mr. Selassie,' I said to him, 'I honestly don't know, but this, what we have seen, this could only have happened here. You made it happen.'

I did not get to hear his response; he was quickly whisked away, hoisted on shoulders and dumped onto the stage.

There was only one possible outcome, Mr. Selassie said, overwhelmed with emotion — they had all won or no one had won. They would divide the cash prize. To make the purse worth it, he was going to add another one million Kenya shillings. Some of the slummers, carried by emotion, pledged thousands of Kenya shillings. If they all came through, the Tizita musicians would take a tidy sum of money home.

Yet, the journalist in me was not satisfied — it felt too easy. Logically, if it was a boxing match, you could rule out The Corporal on a TKO. The Taliban Man was the future that was not yet fully here. So that left Miriam and Kidane. Kidane had invited others on stage, so she too was out on a TKO. That left Miriam. But I also knew no one wanted a winner — not us, the audience, and most certainly not the musicians.

It is hard to convey the feeling at the ABC, so let me put it this way, you cannot divide light; you can trap it, but you cannot divide it; you can work within infinity, but you cannot out-infinite it — an absolute is an absolute, and we had just been given, had shared and helped create, absolute beauty. A once in a lifetime witnessing — no one could win, and no one could lose.

I texted Maaza saying it was a tie. She texted me back: *Love Wins.*

A few seconds later, another text from her: *Tizita Wins.*

I replied:

One day we will be dead and gone
Our graves untended, date of birth
And death from centuries past.
Only our Tizita will remain....

Acknowledgements

This novel would not be alive without the help and interventions from Dagmawi Woubshet and Zerihun Birehanu who helped me listen to the Tizita with my heart; Layla Mohamed and Bibi Bakare-Yusuf for pushing me to the porous borders of my imagination; and to the many (my family included) who let me sink into the Tizita world. I have never believed we write alone. This is a chorus.

Support *Unbury Our Dead with Song*

We hope you enjoyed reading this book. If you think more people should read it, here's how you can support:

Recommend it. Don't keep the enjoyment of this book to yourself; spread the word to your friends and family.

Review, review review. Your opinion is powerful and a positive review from you can generate new sales. Spare a minute to leave a short review on Amazon, GoodReads, our website and other book buying sites.

Join the conversation. If you like this book, talk about it, Facebook it, Tweet it, Blog it, Instagram it. Take pictures of the book and quote or highlight from your favourite passages and share. You could even add a buy link for others.

Buy the book as gifts for others. If you think this book might resonate with others, then please buy extra copies and gift them out on special occasions or just because you want to share the gift of reading.

Get your local bookshop or library to stock it. If you love this book, ask your library or bookshop to order it in. If enough people request a title, the bookshop or library will take note and will order a few copies for their shelves.

Recommend a book to your book club. Persuade your book club to read this book and discuss why you enjoyed it in the company of others. This is a wonderful way to share what you like and help us to boost the sales.

Attend a book reading. There are lots of opportunities to hear writers talk about their work. Support them by attending their book events online and offline. Get your friends, colleagues and families to a reading and show an author your support.

Thank you!

PRODUCTION CREDITS

Transforming a manuscript into the book you are now reading is a team effort. Cassava Republic Press would like to thank everyone who helped in the production of *Unbury Our Dead with Song*:

Publishing Director: Bibi Bakare-Yusuf

Editorial
Editor: Layla Mohamed
Copy Editor: Ibunkun Omojola
Proofreader: Uthman Adejumo

Design & Production
Illustration & Cover Design: Chinyere Okoroafor
Layout: Adejoke Oyekan

Marketing & Publicity
Talent & Audience Development Manager: Niki Igbaroola
Publicist: Fiona Brownlee

Sales and Admin
Sales Team: Kofo Okunola & The Ingram Sales Team
Accounts & Admin: Adeyinka Adewole

MORE TITLES TO ENJOY

Men Don't Cry

Faiza Guene

Pub. Date: 27th July 2021
ISBN: 9781911115694
Genre: Literary fiction

Is it possible to make your own path in the world while upholding your family legacy? That's the question at the heart of this tender and poignant coming-of-age story from the widely-acclaimed author of *Kiffe Kiffe Tomorrow*.

Born in Nice to Algerian parents, Mourad is fuelled by the desire to forge his own destiny. His retired father spends his days fixing up things in the backyard; his mother, bemoaning the loss of her natal village in Algeria. Mourad lives in fear of becoming an overweight bachelor with salt and pepper hair, living off his mother's cooking. When Mourad's father has a stroke, he makes his son promise to reconcile things with his estranged sister Dounia, a staunch feminist and aspiring politician, who had always felt constrained living at home. Now living in the Paris suburbs himself, Mourad tracks down Dounia and battles to span the gulf separating her and the rest of the family.

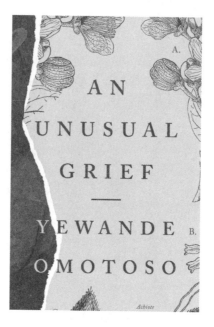

An Unusual Grief

Yewande Omotoso

Pub. Date: 12th October 2021
ISBN: 9781913175139
Genre: Literary fiction

How do you get to know your daughter when she is dead?

When her daughter Yinka dies, Mojisola is finally forced to stop running away from the difficulties in their relationship, and also come to terms with Yinka the woman.

Mojisola's grief leads her on a journey of self-discovery, as she moves into her daughter's apartment and begins to unearth the life Yinka had built for herself there, away from her family. Through stepping into Yinka's shoes, Mojisola comes to a better understanding not only of her estranged daughter, but also herself, as she learns to carve a place for herself in the world beyond the labels of wife and mother.

A bold and unflinching tale of one woman's unconventional approach to life and loss.

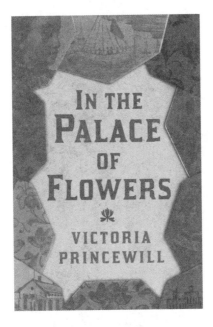

In the Palace of Flowers

Victoria Princewill

Pub. Date: 25th February 2021
ISBN: 9781911115755
Genre: Historical fiction

Set in the opulent Persian royal court of the Qajars at the end of the 19th century, *In The Palace of Flowers* is an atmospheric historical novel following the lives of two enslaved Abyssinians, Jamila, a concubine, and Abimelech, a eunuch. Torn away from their families, they now serve at the whims of the royal family, only too aware of their own insignificance in the eyes of their masters. Abimelech and Jamila's quest to take control over their lives and find meaning leads to them navigating the dangerous, and deadly politics of the royal court, both in the government and the harem, and to the radicals that lie beyond its walls.

Love, friendship and political intrigue will set the fate of these two slaves. Highly accomplished, richly textured and elegantly written, *In The Palace of Flowers* is a magnificent novel about the fear of being forgotten.

A Man Who Is Not a Man

Thando Mgqolozana

Pub. Date: 12th January 2021
ISBN: 9781913175023
Genre: Literary fiction

A Man Who Is Not a Man recounts the personal trauma of a young Xhosa initiate after a rite-of-passage circumcision goes wrong.

This powerful story follows Lumkile's journey into manhood, from crime and violence in Cape Town, to education and first love in the village, and finally to the harrowing isolation of a mountain hut where the protaganist faces the unthinkable and unspeakable.

A Man Who Is Not a Man challenges the code of silent suffering expected of men, and provides a subversive depiction of masculinity, in all its varied forms. Set within South Africa's Xhosa community, this is a local novel with big and universal themes: the confusion of boyhood, trauma, truancy, love, male tenderness and the making of men through violence.

"Highly original." – **Nadine Gordimer**

"His straightforward no-frills prose tells an effective story of a botched circumcision and its consequences." – **Zakes Mda, Sunday Independent**